HEEL

A FEMDOM / MALE SUBMISSIVE BILLIONAIRE ROMANCE

SHANNON ELLIOT

Heel

By Shannon Elliot

Ebook: ASIN B0CD1CMWY8, ISBN 978-1-964117-03-4

Paperback: ISBN 978-1-964117-01-0

First edition September 2023

Second edition March 2025

Authenticity Reading by Book Inc Services.

Edited by Bookcase Media

Edited by Norma Gambini

Cover Art by Clara Stone

Formatting by Shannon Elliot

www.authorshannonelliot.com

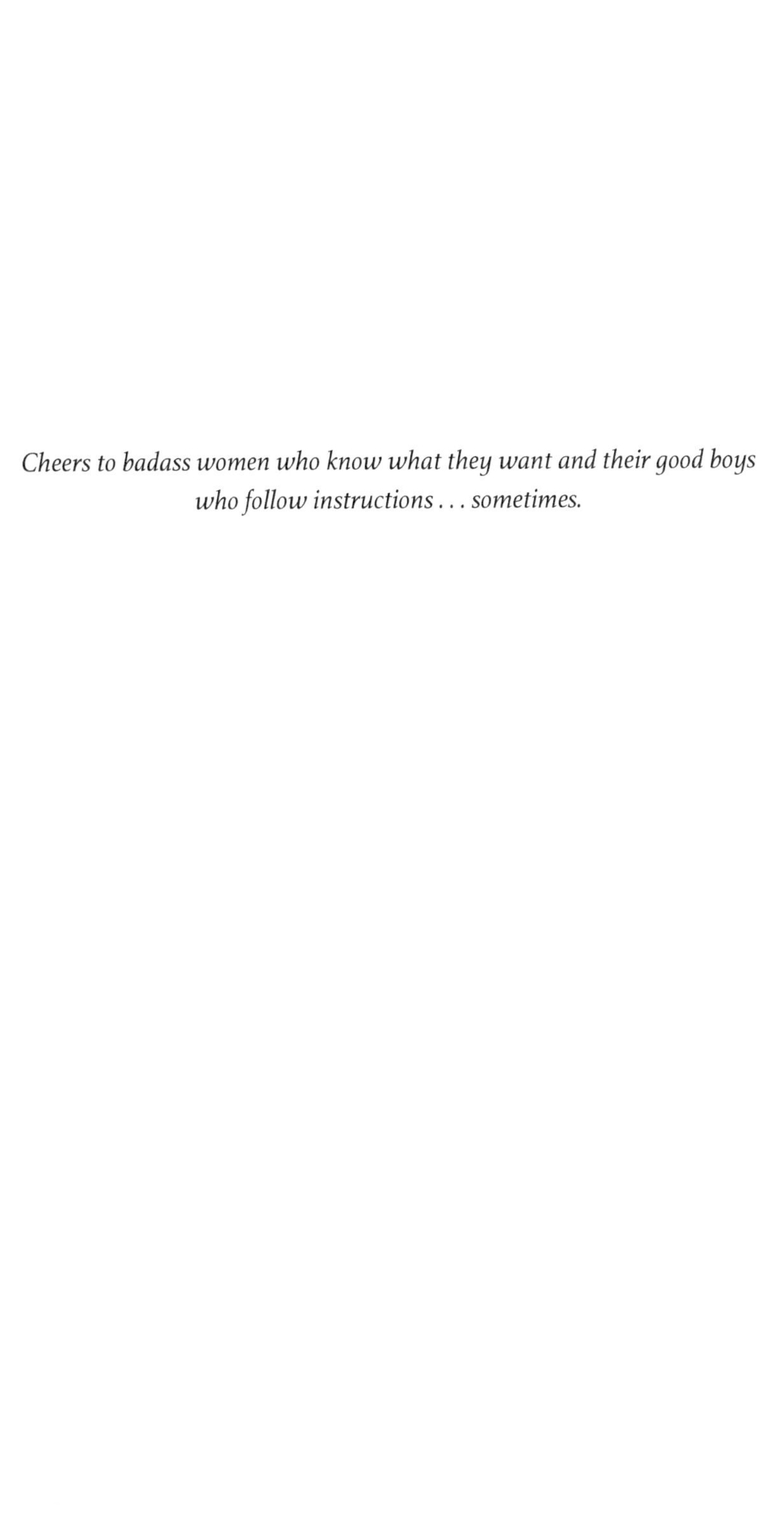

Cheers to badass women who know what they want and their good boys who follow instructions . . . sometimes.

CONTENT AWARENESS

Reader,

Not every book is for every reader, and maybe this book is not for you. Your well-being and mental health come first. So, before diving into this book, I want you to be informed of its content.

Please note this book contains the following: Femdom / Male Sub, Pet Play, Billionaire Romance, Second Chance-y, Spoil me with gifts, BDSM / Kink, On His Knees, Collar / Cuffs, Flogging / Spanking, Edging, Exhibitionism, Degradation / Humiliation, Spit Kink, Punishment / Praise, Aftercare, HFN (Happy For Now), Plus Size FMC.

If you would like further details, have concerns, or feel this list is incomplete, please do not hesitate to reach out to me at authorshannonelliot@gmail.com.

Happy reading!
Shannon Elliot

1

Pet

Each day I've starved for her has been an eclipse.
Daylight shines, but I don't get to experience it, and
darkness pervades, each one emptier than the last.

It's been six and a half months since I last saw my mistress, and
I've been longing for her ever since. She was the brightest moment
in my year, yet I turned away from her like the earth abandons the
sun's light each night.

MONDAY 3:58 P.M.

P: I'm in town this week. If you're around?!

I continue to suffer in silence, enforcing my penance, knowing
I've already done wrong.

MONDAY 8:51 P.M.

P: I'd love to see you.

There have been other people I've fucked since her, but that's
all it is . . . fucking. And I miss it, her. I *crave* her.

P: I wish you were here tonight . . .

Fucking is nothing like the memories we made together. Her hands left streaks of fire on my skin every time we touched. The all-consuming sensation of her lips surrounding my dick and the feeling of her taking me into her warm mouth is burned into my body. I'll never be able to forget her massive cock in my ass and the way her harness dug into my flesh as she pounded into me. The stretch of her inside me undid every stitch holding me together, leaving me fragile and bared for her to see. Any brief moments of release with other partners are nothing compared to the peace and pleasure she wrung from my body, my soul.

TUESDAY 9:43 A.M.

P: Around this week at all?

With each day that passes, I feel even more drained. And now I'm at my wit's end. I'm empty and withdrawn. My desire for her is more necessary than each breath I take.

TUESDAY 6:32 P.M.

P: Mistress? Please, I would really like to see you.

My hunger has me aching for any piece of her after all this time. Desperation will drive a man to do more than beg, and that's what my messages are. They're my outcry for a split second of her attention. I'm frantically holding on, hoping she'll turn her radiance back to me after my regretful neglect.

TUESDAY 7:56 P.M.

M: Next time, remember your manners, and I might respond sooner, pet.

And then there's *light*.

TUESDAY 7:57 P.M.

P: Yes. My apologies, Mistress.

I should have known better, but I was protecting her.

P: May I see you this week before I leave? I'm
here until Friday.

I was a part of crafting our contract. I reviewed every word of the 26-page document with her. But I voided our agreement the second I shunned her. She shouldn't be speaking to me. I don't deserve it, but she seems to have forgiven me anyway.

WEDNESDAY 8:19 A.M.

M: Don't make plans for the rest of the week. I'll
be in touch.

I should have memorized the agreement, studied it until it was burned into my retinas, and could recite it from memory. The words in our agreement meant enough for me to spend countless hours on each of our dates crafting the details of our dynamic. My disregard for their sanctity and her investment in me makes my stomach churn.

I should have tattooed rule number one on my skin as a reminder.

WEDNESDAY 6:54 P.M.

M: Send me your hotel information.

The submissive's role is to please and serve.

Her final directive comes through as I sit in the back of my company car, and a wave of relief crashes over me. I rush to send her all of my information before collapsing against the back of the seat.

"Rough day?" my company driver, Dennis, asks.

"Long," I reply, making my mind recall the dirty memories of sucking on her length. My cock hardens in my pants, and I lean forward to save Dennis from the awkwardness of my evident desire. "But it's looking up. I might get to see a friend while I'm in town."

"Well, that's good," the older man says. "Always nice to reconnect when you can."

"You have no idea," I say with a long sigh.

Walking through the hotel lobby to the elevator bay, I feel the sunshine warm my cheeks for the first time since I lost my guiding star. Even the dim lighting of the cavernous space can't dull the bright, hopeful light in my chest. The ride up to the penthouse floor and the short walk to my suite's door feels like nothing compared to the long inner trials I went through to get here. It's incredible how three messages have the ability to change my entire outlook and brighten even the darkest corners of my heart.

When I get inside, I immediately collapse on the couch in the living room. I should check my email, return my assistant's texts, call my lawyer back, or any of the other hundreds of tasks on my plate. But all I can think about is *her* and how close I am to seeing her radiance once more.

An hour later, there's a knock at my hotel room door. I drag myself from where I still lie and open the door to reveal a petite man with a name tag identifying him as "Wendel." His eyes widen as he takes in my six-and-a-half-foot frame and holds out an envelope with a trembling hand.

Grabbing the lilac and cream envelope, I turn and slam the door shut behind me before collapsing against it and falling to the floor. The note has an elegant "P" written on the front in delicate script handwriting, and I bring it up to my nose to see if I can catch a whiff of her coconut scent. Turning it over, I note the eggplant-purple wax seal stamped with a dove, but I don't hesitate to tear through it to reveal a note and three cards written in the same neatly scrolling handwriting as the front.

~

Pet,

You don't text. You don't call. But you expect me to answer yours like you don't know how we work. Tomorrow, you'll pay for your transgressions in more ways than one.

Enclosed, you will find three cards with hints about my plans. Think of them as two truths and a lie. Only two are punishments, and one is a gift.

Be in the lobby at 6 p.m. tomorrow.

Regards,

M

~

CARD 1:

Lube
Anal Plug
Cock Cage
Cock Rings
Dildos
Collar and Leash
Gag
Rope
Paddle
Flogger
A tribute

~

CARD 2:

> *Your presence is requested at*
> *Brenner's on the Bayou*
> *1 Birdsall Street*
> *Thursday evening, 9:00 p.m.*

~

CARD 3:

> *The Witchery by the Castle*
> *352 Castlehill*
> *December 31*

~

I WAS DISTRACTED ALL DAY, thinking of her. Time dragged from meeting to meeting, yet it still managed to race simultaneously. If I could bring myself to care, it would have been humorous to see my employees fighting to gain my attention. But nothing about the day held any meaning. Instead, I spent my time with my eyes glued to my phone, reading through the finalized contract we both signed all those months ago.

After all our negotiations, I was all in. Or so I thought.

I was riding a high following our last in-person meeting, and my actions were reckless. I was ready to sell my empire and place it at her feet without question. The singularity of her attention made me feel like I could conquer the world for her, and then it all came tumbling down.

One text from the woman I once loved most in this world and everything crashed, making staying away from my mistress and protecting her priority number one.

Phone calls, texts, and emails from my mistress went unanswered, each one adding guilt to my already overburdened shoulders. Then, they progressively came fewer and farther between until, finally, there was nothing but the space in my chest where my heart ached with hollowness.

After that, time slowed to a stop. I was floating in space, no longer propelled forward by my own will or the gravity of her presence in my life.

Until today.

And now, as I sit on the chair in the bedroom, pulling on my shoes, it feels like I'm being knocked back into gradual motion, the grip around my neck loosened, and my freedom slowly being returned.

One glance at the clock tells me I'm running late.

5:56 p.m.

Shit.

I remember the rules by which I am to abide now, having studied them all day, but a part of me knows it won't be sufficient. I'm still new enough, ignorant enough, to the nuances of the lifestyle that I'll indeed fuck this up at some point.

It doesn't really matter how clear she was about her expectations when we first started negotiating. A part of me knows I'll never really be ready for her or adequate.

After twelve years with my ex, my assistant convinced me to try dating apps. I had no idea what I was doing or what I was really looking for anymore—typical for a 28-year-old man—at least not in this area of my life. So, I would download an app and try it for a week before giving up and deleting it entirely. Then, the cycle would continue with new apps or matchmakers or friends of friends. The whole process of "finding love" felt meaningless. Even with partners who appeared to be a perfect fit, there was always something missing, a part of me going unsatisfied.

After all, that's how I got myself into this mess.

I met my mistress on an app recommended by a friend. The app caters to people with particular interests and needs. She messaged me first, and her confidence drew me in. We talked about mundane things for a few weeks, and then she sent me a message that changed everything.

> M: Your profile says you're looking for a dominant partner. What does that mean to you?

I was hesitant to be so explicit about my desires in my bio. Not only because it felt so foreign, but I also wasn't sure how to articulate what I wanted. I tried once before, but I didn't have the words to describe why I wanted to feel unburdened from myself. I didn't have the vocabulary to explain the emptiness I needed to assuage, much less understand what would bring that fulfillment. Jessica left me with so much shame around this emptiness that the best I could do was "looking for a dominant partner," end sentence. So, her question sent me reeling. Yes, I wanted someone to dominate me, but how? How much?

It's like she knew, though. Before I could stumble through an explanation, her following message appeared on my screen.

> M: It's okay if you don't know yet.

And then the final one sealed our fate.

> M: Take me to dinner tomorrow at 7 p.m. I'll send you the address. We can talk then.

The simplicity of the situation felt so natural. I could choose not to go, but I had a chance to meet this magnetic woman while I was in town, and I knew if I stood her up, I wouldn't get another chance.

Porn and fiction don't do dynamics justice. I've quickly realized the whole concept of a dominant and submissive dynamic is widely misunderstood. It can be about what happens in the bedroom, or it can be so much more. It all comes down to negotiating needs, wants, and boundaries.

By the end of our first dinner, I was utterly obsessed. But I needed her to lay everything out for me, to show me how a proper dynamic should work over the following months.

So she did.

Then the guilt and doubt, and my fucking ex-wife, crept in after I left her orbit. And I fucked up.

I am rushing against the clock, knowing I'm already disappointing her. As I descend, my foot taps incessantly against the marbled floor of the elevator car. But the butterflies flying in my stomach aren't fear alone but rather a mixture of fear, anticipation, and need.

"You're late." Her words echo in the empty bay as the elevator doors open.

"Sorry," I mumble, dropping my head.

She says nothing as I lean down and gently kiss her cheek.

Stepping back, I take her in and drool over how her lilac dress cuts low enough to reveal her overflowing breasts, which are barely contained by her lacy bra. The garment is just long enough to be considered modest, barely, but her curves are on full display.

My hands go to her sides, and when I make contact with her full hips, my memory wanders to the image of her fully naked. I move back in, pressing myself close to her, close enough to feel the softness of her tummy, before forcing my leg between her thick thighs. Her feet, clad in matching metallic stilettos, part slightly to let me in, and I'm grateful for the extra six inches they add to her 4'11" frame, so her face is much closer to my own.

Her bright eyes tear into me like they're surveying my entire being for flaws and sins, but then she smiles, and the world disappears.

Mistress is like my own personal sun. I gravitate to her light and joy. She's the only star worthy of notice. I want to worship her, her body, and revolve around it like the center of my universe.

"You're wearing my gift," I murmur, glancing at the sparkling two-and-a-half-carat drop diamond earrings that sparkle in the low light of the lobby, though not as bright as the light shining in her gaze.

"Tribute."

"Yes. Sorry." Her reprimand, the second in my first minutes of seeing her again, stings.

"It's okay. You're rusty," she says, taking my hand and turning to lead me to the hotel lobby. "Did you bring the cards?"

Having partially discerned her instructions, I know we're going shopping and to dinner; thus, I respond, "Yes." My voice trails off, knowing her expectations regarding respectfully addressing her, but I am too embarrassed to admit who she is to me in the hotel lobby and unsure of how else to vocalize my respect for her.

She gives me a curious glance over her shoulder as she leads me out of the hotel, and I wonder how much trouble I'll be in now for not showing her the reverence I owe her.

Outside, the driver, Marcus, I believe, is waiting by a sleek black SUV, but my mistress waves him off when he goes to open the back passenger door. A small clearing of her throat is all I need to prompt me to open the door and hold out a hand for her to settle in.

Her soft hand is warm in mine, and my heart speeds up when I make contact. I soak in the touch, letting it warm my whole body, as she walks gracefully into the vehicle.

Once she's comfortably seated, I close the door and jog around to the other side of the SUV as Marcus starts the engine. When I slid in, I noticed, unlike my company vehicles, there was no barrier between us and the driver.

"Did you figure out any of your clues yet, pet?" Mistress asks before she reaches over to take my seatbelt from me and secures me. Then, she repeats the motions for herself.

I glance up at the driver, pulling out into the street.

"You remember Marcus, right? He is still aware of our relationship dynamic, extremely competent, and very discreet. It's okay he's here, correct?" The reminder of who this man is to us is enough to have me relax back into my seat, and I nod in confirmation at her question. "Now . . ."

Looking over at her, I see her soft features patiently waiting for my answer.

"Yes, Mistress. One is a shopping list. The second is a dinner reservation, which I've gone ahead and confirmed. But the third . . . I'm not sure."

"Good boy," she replies simply before turning her face away to focus on her phone.

The drive is quiet except for the engine's hum and the sound of Mistress's kill-all-men playlist coming through the speakers. Ten minutes later, the driver slows and turns into the parking lot of a black building with no signage. I glance over at Mistress, and a smirk plays across her face. We come to a complete stop right outside the door with blacked-out windows.

"Ready?" she asks, but I'm frozen in place.

My mistress would never do anything to harm me, and I know that. She's pushing me out of my comfort zone and ensuring everyone's needs are met.

"You should open the door, pet. Don't dawdle."

"Yes. Right," I say, fumbling to undo my seatbelt before jumping out of the vehicle.

Any fear I have is overwritten by arousal and need, my desire to please more prominent than any form of shock trying to stop me. I jog around to her door, but she's already halfway out before I can reach her.

"Less delaying next time," she says as I hang my head and follow behind her confident strides toward the double doors. "I'm not a patient woman."

My knees want to buckle at her reprimand, and yet my cock hardens at her stern words. Everything in my body vibrates with want.

The building needs to be more inconspicuous. Nothing makes it stand out among the surrounding businesses. The distinct lack of merchandise or advertisements in the windows makes it seem abandoned, and I'm both excited and terrified to find out what is beyond them.

When we step inside, a black-and-white photograph is suspended from floor to ceiling as we first enter. The woman depicted is tastefully naked. Her thick curves are illuminated by deep shadows and bright highlights of carefully placed lighting. Its placement allows only the briefest glimpse of the store beyond.

As my mistress leads me around the artwork, Wonderland appears. Everything about the space screams luxury. Layered rugs of various colors and textures cover the concrete floor. Someone carefully mismatched all the furniture to create an eclectic but elegant look and feel.

Lingerie is displayed on various racks around the colorful room, and the tables are covered with multiple toys and instruments intended to tempt, tease, and torture. At the back of the store is a platform with a wall of mirrors just beyond. A few changing rooms surround the arrangement, but my mistress stops just in front of the area where couches have been arranged with a perfect view of the central pedestal.

The store manager, Aster, meets my mistress where she stands.

She greets them with a squeal and warm hug before they both jump into a giddy conversation I can only imagine is gossip about their mutual friends. The sudden change in her demeanor gives me the same feeling as when a plane drops midair, and there's a slight sting that I didn't have the same reception. However, witnessing her express such unadulterated joy in the presence of her friends is a gift, and I file away the memory for later.

Mistress and Aster head toward a velvet couch, and another associate, Lily, delivers a Manhattan to her. The motion is seamless between the two, and the glass settles in her hand without sloshing or spilling a drop.

The whole scene happens before me without glancing at me or acknowledging my presence.

Our arrangement makes it clear that I am not to speak to strangers without permission in public. My mistress will take care of me and guide me through all interactions. It's her responsibility to deflect attention and allow me to keep a distance from others I'm generally not allowed to engage with. Typically, my focus is always being demanded by employees, investors, lawyers, and others who see me as a commodity to be used.

If I'm going to be used, it will be with my express permission. And it's going to be by her, my mistress.

Mistress takes a few sips of her drink before politely thanking the assistant.

"At my feet, pet," she commands, placing her drink on the side table. "Don't worry about the others. We have the whole store to ourselves tonight."

"Yes, Mistress," I whisper, immediately kneeling at her feet.

The carpet cushions my knees, but the hard concrete beneath still finds its way through the soft pile. I try to get comfortable where I kneel, but the unknown of what's to come has me restless and twitching.

"Now," she says, running her hands through my hair as she

scrolls on her phone. "I want you to select items to fulfill the list. Consult with the store manager as you must." She pauses, giving me a look to confirm I'm following along. I nod in affirmation before she turns her attention back to her phone. "Good. You will present me with your selections, and then the manager will start preparing for our leave."

I nod, thinking through the list of items in my pocket. "I can do that."

"Keep in mind, these are not for your pleasure but mine. But these items are for you, and I require you to select them yourself. Do you understand, pet?"

"Why?" Her gaze flicks in my direction, and her eyebrows raise at my question. "Umm . . . why are they for me?"

"Because these are personal items. I want you to be comfortable with everything you select. Now, get going. We don't want to be late for our reservation, and I have plans for you back in the hotel room." She looks up from her phone to address me directly. "Oh, and pet? Don't ever question me like that again, or you'll find out very quickly that you might not enjoy being on your knees as much as you think you do."

The next hour and a half is suffocating. The store manager and their assistant are friendly enough to help me find all the selections I need, but the sheer overwhelmingness of the store is nearly painful. Selecting floggers took twenty minutes with all their varieties, and dildos took almost forty-five. There are too many colors, textures, weights, and purposes for each item on her list. And the pleading looks I keep shooting her way, begging her to step in and take away my decision, are ignored.

In every aspect of my life, I am the responsible one, the decision-maker. I'm successful because of this, but I've always craved the freedom to escape the choices I constantly face. It was one of the most challenging parts of the six months I was forced apart from my mistress. I could never let my guard down and let someone else pick up the weight that hung around my neck.

Yet here she is, asking me to take this on myself, to prove I'll do it for her.

When everything is laid out on the checkout counter, exhaustion pulls at my body and mind.

I mentally tally up the purchases as the store manager goes through the items individually. Her body heat presses against mine as they scan each item from behind. Her arms wrap around me, holding me tight around the ribs.

I swallow. "Did I do well, Mistress?"

"Well enough." She sighs. "You followed the spirit of the request rather than the instructions to the letter, but it's fine. It only gives me more to play with."

I looked down at the items on the counter and studied them before realizing I had made choices without ever making a decision.

Three bottles of lube, a silicon, water-based, and synthetic combination, lay on the counter beside a box of anal plugs, plural, in various sizes. The cock cage is adjustable with multiple-size bases, the cock rings are in a set of three, and I chose four dildos of multiple sizes. Even the other assorted items—collars, leashes, gags, ropes, paddles, and floggers—have multiple options on the counter.

"I can . . ."

"No. You made your non-choices. Live with them. There's no room for regret in this world, pet. Regret fogs the mind and rots the soul. Don't let it linger."

I stumble when her warmth leaves me. The click of her heels tells me she's several paces away before she speaks again. "Oh, and pet? You're missing something on your list." She winks as she lifts her phone.

Shit. Her gift, no . . . tribute.

Looking up desperately at the manager before me, I ask, "What do you think she would like?"

They huff. "You should have thought about that while she was still here to ask, boy. Three-thousand, one hundred forty-six dollars, and thirty-two cents," says the manager as I'm fishing out my wallet.

My head whips up at the number. "What?" I stammer, but they just wait. "Right. Here you go," I say, handing over my card.

There's a voice in my head telling me I should be ashamed of spending so much on such frivolous items. It reminds me of all the struggles around money my family had when I was young. But I take a deep breath, knowing I don't live like that anymore, and I'll be more than fine after such a large purchase.

As I'm about to leave with all the bags in hand, the sweet assistant pulls me to the side. "Your mistress likes pretty things, expensive things. There's an exquisite bijou around the corner that I know she frequents as well. A lot of us in the community do because the owner keeps a lot of . . . specific . . . items in stock." She looks at me with a knowing longing in her eyes. "You're rusty. I can tell, but your mistress is kind. Ask for permission and go to the shop. The owner, Edith, lives upstairs and should open up for you if you mention me." They hand me a card.

I stare at the assistant, my jaw unhinged in utter shock. "Thank you," I manage.

Walking quickly from the store to the SUV, I spot Marcus waiting, leaning on the trunk of the vehicle. My heart rate picks up at the sight of his scrunched brow as he scrolls through his phone.

"I need to stop at the jewelry shop around the corner first if that's okay," I explain, praying to whoever is listening that I'm not causing more trouble than I'm worth.

"Not up to me," he replies as he pops the trunk.

With it open, I find my mistress on the phone in the middle

row of seats. The Black man on the screen stops speaking when he notices me, and my mistress's eyes flick to me.

"One moment, sir." She turns to me, looking impatiently over the row of seats. "Yes?"

I know sir—Durante—is her own dominant; they have their dynamic between them, but I've never been able to wrap my head around the idea that my mistress would submit to anyone. Though if there's going to be anyone, he seems like the man to control such a flame as my mistress.

"May I visit the jeweler around the corner, Mistress?" I ask.

"Go," she snaps, waving me off.

Something about her tone is off. There's still command in how she addresses me, but she's holding back.

I want to reach out to her. I want to round the car, throw open her door, and take her into my arms. The impulse is there. But she dismissed me, and in this case, I need to act in accordance with her wishes, much as it pains me to leave her when I can sense the pain emanating from her.

I gently shut the trunk and turn on my heel when Marcus's voice comes from behind me. "It's a smart move. Lily is being generous, telling you about the bijou."

2

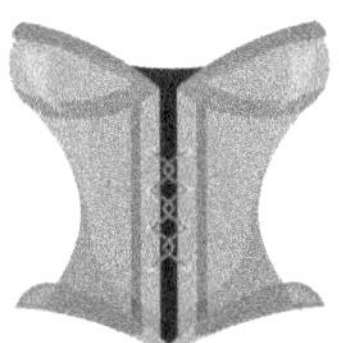

Mistress

Walking out on my pet is rude but necessary. In another circumstance, he'd deserve an apology for my sudden exit, but the ice traveling through my veins isn't what I want to feel. He deserves better than a cold, dismissive mistress to serve.

Pushing through the doors to the parking lot, I'm met with a wave of heat, thawing me a bit. I hit my phone's screen, then bring it to my ear. The shrill ring coming down the line only adds to my oncoming headache. Thankfully, Durante picks up on the fourth.

"Baby bird. What a delight." Durante's bass timber comes through the phone, and tension seeps from my shoulders. "I wasn't expecting a call, though. Don't you have plans?"

The past hour and a half has been grueling despite my efforts to remain detached from the selection process. I kept trying to get lost in my newest book while my pet went about selecting his items with the store's staff, but I struggled to get lost in the world so carefully crafted on my phone. Instead, my attention constantly strayed back to my pet.

My instructions were to make selections and decisions, a task of which I know he's capable. He made a choice when he retreated from me, and now he must make new choices and sacrifices to show his commitment once more. It's part of our void, a negotiated contract that I take care of all public interfacing and decision-making. I would take on these things for him to relieve him of one part of his daily existence and the manipulations he experiences. All because he needs someone to take away the weight of his successful yet stressful life.

But each non-choice made by my pet felt like a personal affront to these instructions and me by proxy, and I just couldn't take it anymore.

I needed some privacy and a minute to regroup and ground myself. I need my sir.

"Sir." I take a deep breath in and out. "I do. He's inside the store, but I left. My restraint is slipping, and I can feel anger trickling in."

When Durante and I first met and formed our dynamic, I had a nasty reflex of lying, or at least withholding my truth, when dealing with messy emotions. My sir, now also my mentor, has always asked me for complete honesty, and lying was a hard habit to break. So, while it hurts to admit internal conflict, this is one of those moments that requires vulnerability once more.

"Oh, baby." He exhales on the other side of the phone. "Switch me to video."

With my pet still in the store, I pull the door open and settle into the SUV. Taking my phone from my ear, I press the screen to add video to the call. As soon as his light-gray eyes shine on the screen, though, my face tightens, and tears well up in my eyes.

"Baby, please don't cry. Take a deep breath in," he instructs, and I inhale. "And out." I exhale.

The lull in conversation is comforting. It's one thing I love about Durante. He never feels the need to fill in silence with wasted words. He simply lets you sit with thoughts and feelings until you're ready to share—ever a therapist. He just waits patiently for me to breathe through my overwhelmed state before prompting me.

"Tell me," he says gently.

My gaze darts away from the phone, the understanding and patience in his expression too much for me to handle. I listen for a minute and hear the distinct sound of a door closing and locking on the other side of the call. When I look back, Durante is leaning back in his office chair, waiting.

I've studied every inch of Sir's face each time we're together, but the sight of him still takes my breath away. His deep brown skin and the curve of his throat teases me as I remember how soft it feels under my lips as I trail kisses along it. My eyes wander over his bulging muscles under his tight dress shirt.

"I . . . I don't know where to start," I confess, fidgeting with the strap of my bag.

Sir has always been my foundation. When I first met him, I was in the darkest place in my life, searching for a shred of hope to cling to. I needed someone to protect me from my thoughts and temptations, dangerous as they were.

Submitting to him was, and continues to be, one of the most freeing experiences I'll ever have. Only my newest endeavor, which he's encouraged from the start, comes close to that level of bliss.

Durante was the one to suggest exploring domination, and he was the first to ever take a position of reverent submission before me. My first experience was with the man who brought me back from my most frightening nightmares and sacrificed so much of his time and himself to ensure I would always feel safe and loved.

That moment will forever stand out in my memory, and my goal is to treat my subs with the same spirit of service he gives me.

"Give me your D.E.A.R., baby. Describe the situation. Express the emotions . . . ," he prompts.

For me, my exploration of domination is not an experience focused on control but instead on service. I want my partners to have a similar experience to my own. I want them to feel free to sink into a place where they can hand over their burdens and the mundane stressors of their lives and entrust them to me.

I've seen my sir on his knees for me twice in our relationship, which was an empowering yet uncomfortable experience. Unlike when my sir went to his knees for me, my pet is a whole different story. Sir looks at me in a way demanding of me, asking for more with each moment in our scene. It is a kind of hunger and lust for a different form of strength compared to my submission.

Pet, on the other hand, looks at me with pure adoration. His attentions feel like a soft comfort and a balm to some of my less healed places. He brings out my need to focus on another person's needs. With him, I channel the part of me that craves not control but care.

I take pleasure in turning his skin red with my flogger, my paddle, and my hand because his submission is hard-won at times. He struggles to let go, and I'm able to provide him with an experience allowing him to release part of his burden. My desire to restrain him and tease him until he's squirming under my attention is because I want to give him release. His success is because of his determination, but his joy and enjoyment of those moments aren't celebrated. Instead, those moments, ones that are vital to remember, are suppressed. Pleasure for him is *work* unto itself.

I take in a few more even breaths before continuing Sir's reminder of the skill he taught me so long ago. "Describe. Express. Assert my needs. Reinforce the boundaries and outcomes."

"Good girl," he says with a smirk, sending pleasure through me.

"I know he's new to this. I know I'm his first formal dynamic, and we only met eight or nine months ago." I start thinking of the repentant looks he's given me tonight when he knows I'm disappointed in him. "He's only 28 and a baby in this world. I know he's learning, but it's so hard to be patient all the time. It feels like my head and heart are in this battle, and no matter who loses, it will hurt."

"Baby, you can know things and still have conflicting feelings about them. Sometimes, you have to allow the dialectic to just be. Two opposite truths can exist at the same time," he says, ever the logical one in our relationship.

"I know. I know."

Sir chuckles in his rumbling rumble, which has goose bumps forming on my skin before falling silent when the trunk opens. Startled by the sudden movement, I jerk my eyes to my pet before flitting back to Sir.

"One moment, Sir," I say, then return to my pet.

Sir is aware of my pet's place in my life, and I know my pet. I've also had extensive conversations about our relationship and dynamic. They've even been introduced on calls, but I know that, fundamentally, my own sir, kind as he is, intimidates my pet.

Like a frightened pup, my pet's eyes go wide, and he freezes.

"Yes?" I prompt, trying to control my tone and expression.

"May I visit the jeweler around the corner, Mistress?" he asks.

I know this is likely about the last thing on his shopping list, my tribute, which makes my mixed feelings boil up.

"Go," I say, waving him off.

I hear when the trunk closes, and there's a slight rock forward of the car when Marcus resumes his post leaning on the back of the SUV, knowing I need a few more moments alone.

When I turn back to Durante, he's smiling.

"He seems eager to please," he says.

"Yeah. Well, he's not doing the best job," I reply dryly.

"Tell me more, baby," he prompts.

As I reflect on the events of the evening, my self-control withers. "I can't tell if it's that he's forgotten our agreement or willful disobedience, but I'm on edge because I feel like he's trying to drive me up a wall with every command I give him."

After setting the phone in the cup holder so I can still see Durante, I drop my head into my hands.

"Look at me when you talk, precious," he commands.

My attention snaps back to Sir.

I've always admired him, idolized him even. His ability to remain calm and levelheaded in any situation is a trait I envy. None of our dynamics has ever appeared to be work. It's just so natural for him, and I fear I may never reach a place where I have the same confidence in my ability.

"How is it so simple for you?" I ask a whine in my tone.

"Well, for one, I'm old and have decades of experience on you." He chuckles. "You're still experimenting with dominance in your first few years, and this boy, pet, is only your second sub." He sighs. "It takes time, baby."

Wringing my hands, I take in his words before continuing, "It'd be so nice to just skip to the happily ever after, though."

There's a part of me that questions whether I even want that. Since he abandoned me, I've had zero confidence in our relationship. I desire him, but do I want him? Is he a person I want in my life long-term, or is this just a bit of fun? All these questions have me bouncing between being willing to put in the effort to make this work and wanting to be done with it.

"Yeah, baby. It would, but that's not how this works, and you know it," he says, his tone firm. "Now, don't get side-tracked. Tell me what happened."

It's moments like this when I crave the feeling of my flogger's soft leather handle in my hand—the strength and surety it gives me. I'm centered and calm, then. My practiced skill shows through, and I know what I'm doing.

That's what initially felt right about my pet and me. He knew my expectations, and I knew his limits. Our discussions were frank and open. The scenes were easy to walk through, with every component flowing flawlessly from one to the other.

So when did it go so wrong? When did communication shut down so severely? How do we go back to before? Do we even try?

"We talked and negotiated for so long before our first meeting, and it went so well, I thought we were really developing some-thing between us. But then he left town again and *ghosted me*," I vent, huffing a breath. "I sent check-in messages and emails, but he never responded. And then he messages me out of the blue again *months* later? I don't deserve to be treated like this."

"You're right," Sir says in the second I take to get air into my lungs.

Righteous anger swells in my chest at the recollection of my weakness. He messaged me out of nowhere, and I relented instead of ignoring his cries for attention. My desire to feel needed won in the end, and I messaged him back. I want him. I need him too much. My thirst for his adoration overpowered the frustration of his disregard. Now, here we are, and I'm paying for my feebleness.

"And what's more! I put aside his dereliction of our agreement and made plans for us after he reached out. I'm putting myself out there again and making plans for New Year's Eve. But then he's late, he doesn't address me respectfully, and he's lazy, indecisive, and inconsiderate. And yes, he apologizes and tries to make up for it ..."

"But he's not perfect. Is that what you're saying?" Sir's smirk only makes me clench my fists.

"Yes! But no. But . . . ugh," I say, letting my head drop back to the headrest behind me.

Pet's apologetic eyes and pouty mouth cross my mind. The softness of his features and the silkiness of his hair makes me want him here with me. I want to stroke and soothe until everything is right again. How he looks at me and always looks at me makes me relax in a way I've only found with Sir. He's a warm blanket wrapped around me on a cold day, a comfort in a chilled environment.

I know how great we could be together, and I want that. But I can't let go of my doubt and fear.

"He's not perfect, and neither are you," Sir reminds me. "Do you remember how many mistakes and fumbles you had initially with Lily? How hard was it for you both to navigate through those? It takes time, precious."

"I know. But I just . . . ," I stammer, not knowing how to explain the ache that's forming in my chest.

"You want the vision in your head," Sir says.

"Yeah," I relent, knowing my vision comes with sacrifices I don't know if I'm willing to make.

But my sir, as usual, I am correct. I want the picture-perfect image in my head. The dream is so close yet just out of reach.

Polyamory isn't always easy to navigate, but having a partner like Durante has made it infinitely easier to learn.

I've talked with Sir before about my ideal polycule. I could never submit to more than one person, though playing with friends occasionally is a totally different subject. But since my curiosity around domination started, I've begun desiring relationships beyond my partnership with Durante, of which he's always been fully supportive. I've always known I want more than monogamy can provide. I don't believe one person is meant to satisfy all of a person's needs. It takes a variety of relationships and dynamics to have a fulfilling life.

In this lifestyle, I'm a person composed of multitudes, and I crave dominance just as much as I desire to submit. I like to think the duality makes me better at each, one nature informing the other. And if the universe is gracious enough to bless me with multiple partners who willingly submit to me? I would be able to die a very happy woman.

My imagination wants to run free with the fantasy, but I need to ground myself in the present.

"Baby, you've done all the intellectual work," Sir says, interrupting my thoughts. "You've studied and learned everything you can about your interests. You are a better Domme than most out there. Your partners are all the better for it, but theory is not the same as practice."

"But I've put in the practice hours," I say, frustrated.

"Yes, you put in the time and effort . . . with Lily," he retorts.

"Exactly!"

"And he is . . ." Sir's patience is clearly running out, and I wince at the sharpness in his voice.

"Not her," I mutter.

"Smart girl." He grins. "Remember. His disobedience is not your doing; it doesn't mean you're losing control of the situation or dynamic. He's what? Seven years your junior? He's young and green. And he's learning. It will take time for him to remember the rules and protocols. That's okay. Just take it at your own pace. Your pace, as in for both of you."

That's the problem, isn't it? I'm impatient and trying to jump ahead, eager to experience the simplicity that comes with truly knowing your partner. This whole situation boils down to whether or not I want to make an effort to build something meaningful with my pet.

Internally, I cringe at the realization that my pet isn't the only one struggling to make decisions today. He's not alone in his journey to find the right path forward. I, too, need to find my way.

"Yes, Sir. Thank you, Sir," I say, more settled than earlier.

"Go spread your wings, baby bird." A knock comes through the phone, and my sir sighs. "One moment," he calls out before returning his attention to me. "Baby, I will always be here when you need me, but you've got this. You know what you're doing." He smiles his full, genuine smile, and I love seeing the joy and pride spreading across his face. "You're a great Domme. If he's the right partner for you, you're lucky to have found each other."

I drop my gaze from him at the praise.

"Eyes up." My eyes snap back up to meet his own on the screen. "You're forgetting the most important part.

"This is play," he says, his smile becoming a smolder. "It's fun. You're supposed to be enjoying yourself. Please don't get so caught up in its minutiae that you forget the complete picture. You're more than prepared for anything that could arise. You're my baby bird for a reason. Go, precious," he finishes before hanging up.

Silence fills the space, and I go to put my phone away when the driver's door cracks open.

"You okay?" Marcus asks as he swings the door wide.

"Yeah . . . Yes. I will be. This just . . . isn't going how I expected," I say, rolling my neck.

Marcus climbs into the SUV and gives me a look in the rearview mirror as he takes his seat before putting the car into drive and starting the drive to the jewelry shop.

"It never does, miss. Never really does." Marcus lets the quiet linger as we make our way around the corner.

Talking with Durante was precisely what I needed. His level-headedness is one of the things I love about him. Without him, I wouldn't be this far on my own journey of dominance. Without his prompting, I probably wouldn't have even considered exploring this side of myself, but it feels right.

When we pull up to the little shop, my pet is already waiting outside with a bag in hand and a broad grin on his face. But something about the cocky look puts me on edge.

"That was a fuckton of money, but the old woman said you would love this," he says as he slips into the car and brashly thrusts the bag in my direction before we start the journey back to the hotel.

My jaw drops at his arrogance. My frustration from earlier rises, and all of Durante's wisdom goes flying out the window. "First off, watch your mouth," I scold. "Second, Edith is never wrong and doesn't deserve your disrespect, nor do I."

Under my scrutiny, his gaze drops, and the arrogant look from seconds ago is wiped away.

I want to comfort him, tell him I know he's trying because I do. I do know, but both of us are volleying between emotions. Tensions are high, and I can't seem to form the calm, patient words I know he needs.

Instead, I lash out. "And, pet? You don't pay for my time, but don't be fooled into thinking there isn't a price to pay for the privilege of my company. A cost which you are welcome to dismiss if you want this to end right here and now."

Financial domination is part of our agreed-upon dynamic, a part he explicitly demanded. You cannot forget our conversations about his upbringing and the guilt he feels about his newfound wealth.

He has the decency to at least *sound* remorseful when he replies, "Sorry, Mistress."

Already, I can see him closing himself off. His shoulders crumple in, and his head ducks down like a turtle retreating to its shell for protection.

I need to stop. I should stop.

But I can't keep the words back before they're out of my mouth. And I'm not releasing him back to his devices easily. "Are you, though? You've done quite a bit of apologizing tonight, but I don't think it's sincere."

I stare at him when he looks up, waiting for him to acquiesce and drop his gaze in submission. He tries to hold out, but when he finally succumbs, warmth spreads through my chest.

"It is, Mistress. I'm deeply sorry." The words are mumbled enough that I can't tell if they're sincere. He can't even vocalize his apology correctly, and it makes me snarky.

"You will be." I huff, smirking at him.

"Would you like your gift now, Mistress? I promise I didn't look. The shopkeeper said I shouldn't ruin the surprise but that you would love it," he asks tentatively, once again pushing the bag in my direction.

"Stop." I snap. "Down."

He freezes, eyes wide on me when he looks up at me.

"Keep it. I don't want it." It's as though he fades further before me, and a part of me wants to feel bad about my assertiveness. So I soften a bit, not wanting him to hate me. "Not like this."

"Not like what?" he asks.

"This," I say, gesturing between the two of us. "This whole situation is fucked up, and your shiny trinket will not make it better."

If I know Edith, she chatted with him for the thirty minutes I was away and learned enough about him to find the perfect tribute. It would be exquisite in construction and flawless in beauty, as are all of her fineries. There's not a single person in the lifestyle who doesn't know, or at least learn of, her impressive ability to sense what is needed. She knows sometimes before you do. It's spooky.

"What will fix it, Mistress?" There's a slight tremble in his voice, and I hate the sight of him fighting back emotions. I want him to feel free to be open with me, yet here I am, making him feel, once again, like I'm another person he needs to shield himself from. Such a strong man, strong enough to willingly submit, shouldn't cry, not because of me. "Please, tell me what I've done wrong, and I'll fix it. I want to be good for you."

"Right. Good." I sigh, tired. "You want to be good."

"Please, take it. Accept it as my apology for whatever I've done wrong." He looks so earnest, and the sentiment is sweet, but I need more from him.

"I don't want your apology, trinket," I snap, which gets his full attention. "I especially don't want a meaningless blanket apology."

"What do you want, then?" he says, his chest puffing up as his indignation rises.

A long moment of silence passes while I consider what I genuinely want after the events of the day.

I've given him a second chance simply by being here, seeing him again, *trying* again. And he's wasting it.

What's more, I've already planned what is supposed to be a magical getaway for the two of us in the new year. But right now, the thought of traveling across the Atlantic for this man makes my heart stop.

"I want card three." I hold out my hand, waiting for him to hand over the card.

"What?" he asks.

"My gift to you, card three. I want it back." I look away from him, my hand still outstretched in expectation.

"What?" he repeats.

"Don't play daft, pet. Hand it over." It takes a moment, but I feel it when the weight of the card hovers just above my palm. It's like he's struggling to let go. Finally, the card drops fully into my hand, and I pull it away from him without looking back. "I hope you learn your lesson from this."

"What?"

I'm barely withholding rage at this point. I can't hear the sincerity in his voice, so surely he's only playing the fool, which makes my head spin.

"You might as well stop speaking at all if you're just going to play like a broken record," I snap before taking a deep breath. "I'm saying . . . let this be a lesson to you. Punishment and reward come in many forms. I planned a gift for you, but you're clearly not worthy of it. And just like you will have to earn back my gift, you will also earn the right to pay me tribute."

"I just don't understand. What did I do?"

Something snaps in me at his insolence. "Your irreverence over the past months is a loathsome way to treat someone, especially me. I've given you another chance, pet. And your behavior for the past few hours has been abhorrent. You're blowing it."

Sputtering is all that comes out of his mouth at my censure, but my annoyance has taken over. In the window's reflection, I can see how he's pressed himself up against the car door. He's retreating from me when all I want is to have him close.

Shame lies heavy in my chest at the thought of him being afraid of me, but I'm a train wreck, and there's no stopping my self-destruction.

"Shut up and give me a moment to center myself before I really get angry with you," I say, trying to calm myself down. "You *don't* want me to be angry."

Buildings pass by as I look out the window, but my attention is truly on the reflection of my pet's expression. He looks devastated, and my heart aches for him, but I can't help all the feelings he brings up in me.

He simultaneously makes me feel irrationally adored and endlessly frustrated. I love the way he looks at me, but I loathe the way he speaks to me.

"I like you. You must know that. But do you know what I think of when I look at you now?" I whisper, tears forming in the corner of my eyes. "I see your inadequate attempts to gain my favor and can only think of how pathetic you are." I choke back tears and center myself, focusing on the part of me desiring to break and reform this man into an image he can be proud of. "Your place as a man is destroyed in my eyes. You're less than a mutt."

He's wide-eyed when I turn to face him, but he takes the degrading endearment in stride. "Yes, Mistress. I'm a mutt."

"That's a good pet," I smirk at the glimmer of pleasure in his eye. I recognize that look. It's a look saying more, harder, deeper. It's his desire to have me push him further, to his limits, to explore this kind of play we've only discussed in theory. "You're not worthy of licking the dirt off my stilettos, much less of being my sub."

He was such a good boy before and never deserved harsh and insulting words. But now, he's earned them, and they flow naturally from my tongue. And he *wants* them.

"Pet. Darling." I let him see a bit more of the fear haunting me. "Your wealth, your billions, they are nothing to me. Your obedience is my real gift. Nothing compares to your submission. And until you've proven to me you truly want this dynamic, I don't want your tribute."

The same heavy heartache overcomes me as I look out the window and find we're approaching the hotel once more.

"I just want you," I whisper, glancing back at his devastated expression.

"I . . . ," he tries.

"Don't speak to me. Pets don't talk." I sigh. "Apathy is the worst kind of death, Pet. Because apathy means I'm past caring, you are dangerously close to the line."

At last, we turn into the hotel roundabout, and the valets open the doors for us to exit. I wave away the men, signaling for him to close the door, before looking to pet, who's still sitting in his seat, awaiting directions.

"Grab my things from the trunk along with the shopping bags. Bring them upstairs. Unpack everything. Then make sure you're ready for me. Collar and leash on for when I arrive. I'm going to take some time for myself before joining you."

"Yes, Mistress," he says softly as he climbs out of the car. "I'll do better. I promise."

"Yes, you will," I reply. I can't bear looking at him right now, so

I focus my gaze on the front and meet Marcus's eyes in the rearview mirror. "Marcus, please, I need to go to the grocery store."

3

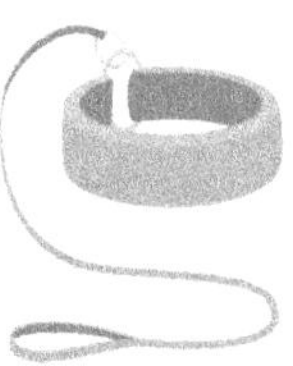

Pet

My ex weaponized her words in the last months of the divorce. Words can be cruel, and she used them as her tool to cut at me until I was bleeding. For years, she tried to find something to hurt me in the proceedings, and then she did.

Six months ago.

Six months ago, my ex found out about my mistress. She learned I found someone who accepted me for my needs and desires instead of shaming me, and she armed herself with the knowledge to take everything from me. But her indiscretions were enough to make a judge see reason in the end. Her ending was a new beginning for me, a new dawn drawing me back to where I belong, with my mistress.

During the negotiations of our arrangement so many months ago, I had marked degradation as a "maybe" on my list. It was something that intrigued me, but I'd never had experience with it before. Every day, I have yes-men at my side, and a particular exhaustion comes with constantly being praised when you know you don't deserve it.

But my mistress has never spoken like that to me before. We'd discussed it, but she said it wasn't her thing. She said she would degrade me if it was something I really wanted, but it wasn't natural for her.

But then . . . *mutt.*

Hearing her call me that, having it slip so flawlessly from her lips, it did something to me. A new warmth spread through me at the endearment, though it wasn't intended as one. There was a possessiveness there I missed. In one word, she claimed me as hers, even though I knew she was only trying to protect herself.

It hadn't crossed my mind that this singular woman now plays such an essential role in my universe. I was living on a high after my last encounter with my mistress. It took me far too long to realize why the darkness took over again after I left her, why it felt so much emptier.

My heart aches for the hurt I've caused, and I will do anything to repair the damage. I ignored her, neglected her, for far too long. Now that I'm back in her orbit, I need her light, her warmth. I'll take any piece of her I can get, even if it means licking the dirt off her heels. Sure, she was lashing out, and I pushed her to the point, but her attempt at making me feel small made me feel *seen.*

I'm not worthy of her, but she chose me anyway. That's what it means to be her mutt.

To the best of my ability, I've tidied the luxury room, double-checking that I unpacked everything from our shopping trip. I've straightened everything multiple times, adjusted it to sit just so, and then returned it to its original state.

Though I'm hesitant to unpack the bag she brought, I want everything to be perfect for her.

Looking around, I take in the extensive suite my assistant booked me into. The modern lines of the room are pleasing to the eye. White linens contrast with the dark brown wood of the furniture. The split living and kitchen area hosts a comfortable couch, perfect for cuddling . . . or more nefarious activities. Everything is tastefully done, though more extravagant than I need yet less than my mistress deserves.

I'm grateful for my wealth. It's given me opportunities beyond my wildest imagination, allowed me to grow my businesses and investments, and allowed me to travel and live in luxury. However, there's an emptiness that comes with money—a loneliness.

My heart seizes when I glance at the clock next to the bed.

8:12 p.m.

It's only been thirty minutes, and yet it feels like forever.

Her curt dismissal in the car stung, leaving me desperate to make things right.

A slight knock, just three little raps, comes from the door, and I use my long stride to get to it. I swing it open to reveal my mistress, and I'm struck silent by how incredible she is and how lucky I am to be in her vicinity.

"Are you ready for me?" She raises an eyebrow. "Or is there something you need to rectify before I enter?"

My hand goes to my throat, remembering her directive to be wearing a collar and leash when she arrived.

Panicked, I let the door swing shut in her face, immediately cringing, knowing how pissed off she'll be at me for the display of disrespect. But I quickly go over to the table where I've laid out all of my purchases. Instinctively, I grab the violet collar made of soft leather and its matching rose gold leash and turn to rush back to the door as I put it on around my neck.

Opening the door once more, I'm met by a scowling, tiny woman.

"Sorry, Mistress. I'm sorry," I spit out before she delivers the scolding I deserve.

"Yes. Well . . . you have a lot to make up for tonight," she says tersely, pushing past me.

Her confident strides into the room put an enormous distance between us. I scurry after her just to stay in the vicinity of her radiance.

She takes in the table of offerings I've laid out for her before turning to me, another frown on her face.

"You didn't unpack my bag," she comments.

"I," I stutter. "I wasn't sure . . ."

She lets out an exaggerated huff, and I'm grateful for its playfulness, as evidenced by the crinkle around her eyes.

"Unpack everything means *everything*, pet," she scolds, and I jump to follow her orders.

As I open the bag, my heart swells. A garment bag, shoes, a packing cube with silk pajamas, and a toiletries tote are on the top.

She's saying the night.

I let out a relieved breath and continued to unpack, pulling out very familiar items from our last encounter. Carefully, I lay out the two floggers on the table alongside a leather paddle. The feel of the instruments, as they drift through my hand, reminds me of the pleasure and pain she uses as a balm on my broken soul—the pure bliss and contentment she can drive me to.

I can feel her presence beside me as I organize everything, but my gaze snaps to her when she reaches for the tie on her dress.

"Take everything out of the packaging," she says, undoing the bow at her waist and letting the dress fall open to reveal a set of lacey lingerie. "Clip off any tags and throw them all away. Then, I need you to wash all the toys and bring them back, along with a towel."

There's a slight tremor in my hand at the command in her voice. I go through the movements to remove everything from its packaging and break the boxes. I clip the plastic tabs off with a pair of nail clippers from my toiletries bag before sorting all of them. All the while, my mistress stands in the center of the room, watching me wander frantically back and forth in the suite.

I want her to take over and walk me through every step, but the smirk on her face makes me think she's enjoying my flightiness.

She's planted her feet shoulder-width apart, and her arms rest behind her back, hands clasped. She looks regal with her head held high as she observes me. Every glance I risk in her direction causes me to falter in my actions before I'm able to gather myself and refocus.

It takes me several trips back and forth between the table where all the toys lay and the bathroom where I wash them all. Each item I handle has my body vibrating in anticipation, knowing how capable each is of inflicting a variety of responses from me. My hands shake as I wash the set of plugs I selected, each larger than the next. My ass clenches at the thought of having one of them deep inside me. The dildos, too, vary in length and width, and I can't help but think of the exquisite feeling they'll have on me as she drives them deep into my hole.

I never knew washing sex toys would bring up so many heart-felt emotions, nor did I think the process would be such a turn-on, but as I dry off the cock rings I selected, my dick perks up in attention.

She studies me as I move, and there's a softness there that I've been missing. Every slight smirk gives me hope I've done well, but there's a lingering doubt I'm still not enough for her. Trepidation threatens to swallow me as my mind races to try and guess what she's thinking.

Am I moving fast enough for her, accomplishing the tasks she set out for me in the way she wanted? Is she judging me for my movement, speed, manner of navigating the room, and task? I want to be worthy of her care and attention. I want to earn back what I know I lost six months ago.

When I'm done washing and drying my new toys, I return to

her, arms laden with the instruments of my pleasure and punishment.

"Lay every item back out on the table. Group them appropriately," she says when I've finished.

I return to the table with all the toys, but just as I've set down the last item, there's a jerk on my collar, which has me stumbling back. I nearly fall to the floor, but my mistress is there to catch me, my leash clasped in her hand. She turns her wrist to wrap the chain around her fist and tugs up, forcing my chin to rise.

"And, pet? You forgot your towel," she teases.

My jaw clenches at yet another scolding, well deserved as it is, and I rush to grab towels.

When I return, my mistress is sitting on the edge of the bed, clad in her lingerie. The lace of her matching bra, thong, and garter belt set has my mouth watering and my mind wandering. The set is a pink floral lace with detailed embroidery, making her look like a fairy.

My fingers itch to touch her, to run my thumbs along the skin beneath her bust and trail the pads of my fingers along the top seam of her thong where her stomach is softest.

If I had my way, I would get on my knees and worship her body, every inch of skin, all of her stretch marks, dimples, and scars. I would pull aside the strip of fabric covering her pussy and bury my face into her cunt, committing her taste to my memory.

When my eyes return to meet her own, she has a broad grin, as though she knows exactly where my thoughts journeyed to.

One glance down has me shifting my attention to one of the smaller plugs I purchased. She holds it between her fingers by the base like a cigarette, and her wrist drops back in that way, which makes me think of those glamorous women in film noir movies.

"Lay out the towel and get on the bed on all fours," she says when my attention comes back to her. "Ass in the air, shoulders pressed into the bed. Present for me, pet."

"Yes, Mistress," I say, breathless at the image of my body twisted into position for her to have access to my ass.

When I approach, she pats the space next to her, and I carefully lay down the towel. My anxiety has me tugging at the corners to get it just right, hoping to prolong the moment a little longer.

In a second, my fantasy and reality collide. It's been such a long time since I've given anyone access to my body like this. I want to trust her again, but a small amount of fear slips into my thoughts. So I just stare at the towel laid out on the bed.

"You're stalling," she quips.

"Of course, Mistress," I reply quickly and scramble onto the bed on all fours.

My body is tight, waiting for the moment when she'll touch me. When she finally does, I can only feel the faint warmth of her fingertips through the lightweight wool of my suit pants. Then I feel the full warmth of her body as she wraps her arms around me.

"You're wearing quite a lot of clothes. Aren't you, pet?" She purrs into my back before her hands caress my abs through my dress shirt and trail down to my belt buckle. "I think I should take care of that problem, shouldn't I?"

"Yes, Mistress," I breathe, trying to calm myself.

The clink of my belt buckle sends a chill down my spine. Then I feel her fingers dip beneath my waistband to undo my fly. Her touch travels to my sides, where she digs her fingers into the fabric and pulls down on my pants and boxer briefs, exposing me.

"Oh, pet. Look at you," she says, trailing her hand over my ass and squeezing. Her nails bite in just enough to give me a glimpse of what tonight will bring. "What a pretty boy you are."

She takes a second to straighten the fabric around my knees, her need for order interjecting itself into the moment. Then, a chill rips through me as her fingertips scratch up the backs of my bare thighs.

"Relax and push your shoulders into the bed. Keep your ass in the air," she says, her hands leaving my thighs and trailing down my spine.

She takes her time, caressing every inch of my body. Her hands roam under my shirt to let her nails rake against my pecs and abs. The tingling sensation has my body vibrating with adrenaline. Then they trail over my hips and back to my ass, where she massages me.

"Mistress, please," I plead.

"Please, what, pet?" she says, a smile in her voice.

Everything about our relationship is a back-and-forth, a parlay between parties. She told me in the beginning that negotiation never ends and communication should always remain open. But all of that requires knowing what you want. And what is that, really?

"Pet, if you want something, you must use your words," she remarks.

Do I want a release? No. Not really. I want her attention. Her focus centered just on me. I want *her*.

I pant, trying to form coherent thoughts. "Please, Mistress. I want your cock in my ass."

The desire to belong to her, to have her use me for her enjoyment, is stronger than any personal need to feel myself tip over the edge of bliss.

Over my shoulder, I see her pick up the plug once more, and my body tightens. "Mmm. You do, do you? You want me to fill you up with my cock and pound into you until you have bruises from where the buckles dig into your ass?"

I recall each of the dildos I cleaned: the purple eight-inch one with a prominent head and veiny length, the six-inch-thick flesh-colored one that had me dreaming of being choked on cock, or maybe the six-inch vibrating blue dildo which makes my ass clench just at the thought of how good it would feel to have her use it on me.

"I don't think you deserve it, though," she says, placing the plug back on the bed. "Good boys get rewarded but misbehave, and you receive your punishment in kind. And you haven't been a good boy, have you, pet?"

"No, Mistress. I've been so bad," I reply, turning my face down into the sheets.

Her hand runs up my spine underneath my shirt, and I soak up the warmth of her touch and the glory of her attention. They stop at my shoulders, and then her nails rake down my spine.

"You really have. But do you know what you've done? What are you responsible for?" I hesitate to answer her, knowing my list of "grievances" is long but unsure what comprises it. "Don't lie to me, pet. You've already done enough damage for the evening."

I take a breath and think through our time together thus far. I try to recall the contract I reviewed all day, but the feel of her hands on my body makes everything fuzzy and far away. Her touch continues to trail all over my body, distracting me from my efforts to remember what I've done wrong, how I've disrespected her, but it doesn't come.

"No, Mistress. I know I've been bad, but I don't know what I did," I say, heavy shame blanketing my body.

"Oh, pet," she scolds.

Her hands leave my body, and I desperately want to follow her as she moves, but my instructions were to look down, to bury my face in my shame. I want to do better for her, at least in this.

"I hoped you wouldn't say that. You were such a good boy once," she recalls wistfully. "But you've been misbehaving all night. I thought you might remember the better man you were then by now. Clearly, you're still struggling to recall how we work, though, aren't you?"

I can sense her hurt, though I can't see her face. I hadn't hoped, per se, she found our separation as painful as I did, but it's clear I did damage when I vanished from her life. Yet, the walls surrounding my complete submission are still built up high.

"I thought I would punish you after dinner for disappearing on me, but it seems you need some corrections for your transgressions now, don't you?" she says, her voice fading as she moves away from me.

There's a rustling from behind me before a scraping sound reaches my ears, and the smell of freshly peeled ginger fills the room, burning my nose.

"Do you remember what I told you is one of my favorite punishments?" Mistress says from behind me, her heels softly falling to the ground as she kicks them off.

I think for a moment about all our discussions and negotiations. "Fuck. The ginger thing?"

A harsh swat lands on my ass, and I realize my mistake. The sting radiates through me, making me wince in pain. And yet, I want more.

"Sorry, Mistress. I apologize for my language," I say.

"Mmmh. Better," she says, and I break out into a smile hidden by the sheets I've buried my face into. "Yes, the ginger thing." The air vibrates with both her excitement and my nervousness. "It's called figging, and right now, you're going to get your first taste of it."

Fear says I should say no. Part of me says I don't want this, but the other, more buried, part says I deserve this. Whatever Mistress has in store for me is precisely what I deserve. And this new experience is worth it if it brings her satisfaction.

My stoplight colors are on the tip of my tongue, but I push through the fear and give into my mistress's will.

"Yes, Mistress," I relent.

There's something so freeing about giving in, just letting her take over, and knowing she has my best interests at heart.

A dominant's most incredible honor is taking away the pain of the present and protecting her sub from anything that could harm them. Anything, pet. Do you understand that?

She told me those words with all the seriousness of a vow so many months ago, forever emblazoning them upon my soul. It's what makes it so easy to say yes to her. I know she would never hurt me. She's my safeguard, the barrier between me and the rest of the world.

"Yes, pet. You're going to take what I give you and then beg for more."

Her hand returns to my lower back, and I relax into her touch and words. "Yes, Mistress."

Her voice hardens. "Or we part, and you get nothing."

Anxiety strikes in my chest, but the gentle caress she trails over my ass has me surrendering once more. "Punish me. Whatever you think I deserve."

A kiss at the base of my spine has a pitiful moan spilling out of me before I can stop it.

I know I deserve to be punished, I've got plenty to make up for, and I want to willingly take all she has to give. There's still the underlying fear that comes with enduring it.

We've discussed punishments in the past, but we never had a need for them before. It's as though our time apart has made me more combative, more deserving of her discipline.

"You're going to take this from me, no complaint. Got it?" she says, looking for confirmation.

"Yes. Please. I can take it," I answer honestly.

Cool gel slides down the curve of my ass before I feel a new sensation prod at my puckered hole. There's a slight sting as my mistress uses the ginger to rim my asshole. Then, the sensitive tissue tightens at the searing sensation it sends through me when she pushes it in.

Clarity transforms me as the sensations from the ginger

radiate through my body. It's like the haze from the past six months, the zombied man I was, just falls away.

I remember all the times I spent my days with my mistress, talking to her and giving her everything she deserved. The evenings we spent cuddling and whispering ideas and dreams to each other come rushing back.

The ginger thrusts deeper into me, and the sensation increases tenfold. I can feel how deep it is, and I hiss as the pain sears through every nerve in my body. As the sting radiates through me, the hardened shell that formed around me at the end of my divorce cracks and disappears under the weight of my punishment, my submission.

Lightly, she presses the ginger farther into my ass before pulling it out ever so slightly. She repeats the process over and over until I'm writhing in agony. Every nerve in my body is on fire, yet I sink into a new, fully encompassing sense of safety.

And then everything stops, the ginger she left still buried inside me.

"Good job. You took this so nicely for me," she coos, rubbing her hand in circles against my ass. "Now, we have 20 minutes before we need to leave for dinner. You'll sit here for five and take your punishment. Got it."

My brain is hazy with pain, but I manage to nod to her. The pain is worth it, though, for she sits next to me, her hand stroking up and down my body the entire five minutes I push through her punishment. I whimper through the pain as she caresses me. The soft tingle of her fingertips on my skin so strongly contrasts the torture of the ginger in my ass that it makes the whole process almost worth it.

"One more minute," she encourages, just as tears form at the corners of my eyes. "You can do this. You're stronger than you think, pet." Her fingers rake into the hair at the base of my neck, and she tugs tightly at the strands. "Breathe through it. In for ten, then hold, and out for ten."

Dutifully, I follow her instructions, breathing as she counts for me. After a few solid gulps of air, my body relaxes, and the pain from earlier transforms into a warm numbness. Just as I'm sinking into the sensation, she stops counting.

"Good job, pet," she soothes.

A tug at the ginger in my ass sends another shock through me as she works it back out of me. By the time she fully removes it, I'm breathless and panting, but the prickling I thought would have dissipated almost seems worse now.

"Shit." I hiss.

"Language," she scolds, giving me yet another smarting on my ass.

"Yeah. Sorry," I apologize, rocking back fully onto my heels into child's pose. Thankfully, she doesn't comment on my change of position.

"Can you take more?" she says, running the back of her hand down my spine once more and rubbing soothing circles on my ass.

"More?" I ask, my voice trembling.

My ass clenches at the idea of taking the ginger yet again, but when I look up at her, she's practically glowing.

She says simply, "I want to go out to dinner with you wearing a plug for me."

"As punishment," I state, rocking back to a kneeling position.

"No, not as a punishment. You've taken enough for now, but you'll receive the rest of your punishment later." She cracks her knuckles thoughtlessly. "This is for pleasure: both mine and yours. I want you to squirm at dinner the whole time. I want you to be stuffed all evening so that by the time we come back here, your cock will be weeping for my own. Can you do that?"

"Yes." I pant. "I can do that. I want it."

She smiles, and it brightens my world. The darkness that's consumed me dissipates, and I cling to the light she brings.

My connection to this woman has always been natural and innate. Until today, we've never really struggled to connect, everything flowing so easily between us. But even this new dynamic between us makes it feel like I'm being drawn closer to her.

"Get back down on the bed." Her voice is cool and even, but all the tension from earlier is gone. Instead, her hand moves to rest on my thigh, and she addresses me almost lovingly. "This may sting a little bit at the beginning because of the ginger you just took, but the lubricant should help calm things down."

I nod and return to my position on the bed, but I need to get a final confession off my chest.

When I turn to her, she's looking at me curiously. "Umm. Mistress?"

"Yes?" she replies, pushing gently on my shoulder to maneuver me into position.

"You said I should always be honest with you," I say, relaxing back down into the mattress and turning my head to the side so I can still see her.

"I did," she says, reaching for my cock to give it a few strokes.

All thought flees as I revel in the feel of her palm around me. Her firm grip has me hardening in her grasp, and I let out a deep moan as she works me over while my body fully relaxes into her touch.

"I liked it," I confide, remembering my original train of thought.

"Liked what, pet?" she says curiously. "The ginger?"

It takes me a moment to gather myself again. All my mistress has ever asked of me is honesty, and I can't keep this from her. If I want more, then I need to be brave enough to ask.

"No. I like it when you say those things about me," I confess.

"What things?" She's teasing me and my cock simultaneously. "Use your words."

"I liked you calling me mutt," I confess.

"Hmmm." She hums as she drags her free hand down my spine, letting her hand rest on my ass in the end. "So if I told you you're going to take this plug for me? Knowing your worthless little hole is just a place to get fucked? And what you have between your legs . . . It's mine to control."

"Yes, Mistress. I'd want that." I pant out.

Mistress's hand strokes over my ass before placing a hard smack against my already sensitive skin. The sting reminds me of the pain I just endured and the punishment I took for my regrettable behavior today.

"You're going to wear it all night for me. We're going to sit in the restaurant, and as you order, you're going to squirm under the waiter's attention. They won't know quite what's going on, but they'll know how depraved you are."

Her reprimand makes me shiver, yet a part of me preens, proudly knowing I'll do this completely at her will. I'm hers to play with, and this is the price she's asking me to pay.

Mistress takes the plug and slathers it with lube before tracing it up and down the divide of my ass. The cool gel soothes some of the earlier pain, all the while enhancing the lingering heat left by the ginger, like aloe on a sunburn.

"Are you ready for me, pet?" she asks as she places the tip of the plug at my puckered entrance.

"Yes, Mistress. Please, I need it."

I groan as she starts pushing into me, loving the fullness it brings.

Then she stops, the plug only halfway in, and I let out a needy, high-pitched whine. "Yes, pet. Moan and whine like the sissy you are. Cry out because I'm the best thing to happen to you in your shitty life."

Slowly, she resumes teasing the plug in and out of my ass. The ginger from earlier has already stretched me just enough to make this not painful, but each press of the plug into my back channel has me gripping the comforter tightly, trying to tamp down my urge to move away.

"You'd do well to remember that the next time you're with one of those bitches you sleep with when we're apart," she says, reaching around to tease my cock as she presses into my ass. "You have been with other partners since we last got together, correct?" Lightning shoots through me at the dual sensations which are over-loading my system. "Did you let them use you like I do, pet? Or have you just been having vanilla sex with boring, faceless partners?"

Her tight grasp on my cock, working its way up and down my shaft, has me biting my raw lip, trying to hold back from the edge of release.

"Just vanilla sex, Mistress. But I finger my ass and think about you." I gasp out into the comforter.

"Mmmm. You must be so needy for my cock then," she teases, withdrawing the plug from my ass completely.

"Please," I keen.

The sudden emptiness leaves a hollowness in my chest. Being full for her is a privilege, and now that's taken away from me.

I want it back. I want to be back in her good graces and worthy of her.

"I think tonight I'm going to fuck your face and have you choke on my cock until you cry before I fuck you in the ass," she taunts, giving my ass a quick smack.

"Please, Mistress. I need more. I need cock so bad." My begging is desperate. All I want is to feel her consume me, every part of my being. I want to be filled with her. I want my cock buried in her warm pussy. I want to feel her everywhere. "I want you to fuck me in the ass and the face at the same time."

"I'll have to think about the logistics of how we can make it work." She hums. "Never say never, though."

Her hand strokes soft circles on my ass. I feel the coolness of more lube depositing at my back entrance before she speaks. "Do you think you can take it, pet? Can you take this whole plug for me?"

The moan I let out is embarrassingly high-pitched and whiny, but I pant out a response. "Please. Yes."

Pressure at my entrance returns. My chest sinks farther into the bed, and I bury my face in the comforter as she works the plug in and out.

The fullness is incredible and all-consuming, but it's the sensation of having my mistress's full attention. Her singular focus has me writhing on the bed, pushing back and desperate for more. My body hums with the thrill of how she coaxes every response from me.

"Take it for me like a good boy," she says with a purr. "Take it for me like you'll take my cock."

"Please. I need it," I beg, needing the torment she's inflicting on my ass to cease.

Then, her movements stop completely before she pushes the rest of the plug into my ass. The force of the intrusion has me rocking forward, and I collapse.

"There you go. Good job. You're such a good slut for me, taking your plug like this," she praises.

"Thank you, Mistress." I moan, feeling the flared base of the plug trapped tightly between my cheeks.

"On your back, you flea-ridden mutt," she commands, swatting my ass before gripping me by the shoulder and tossing me onto my back.

Next thing I know, my cock is back in her hand, and she's stroking me up and down like she wants me to come. But before I can get close, she slips a cock ring around my head and pulls it down so it wraps around my base and balls.

"I want you to be hard all night, pet. You're going to struggle to hide your needs from the valet, the hostess, the servers, and the manager at the restaurant. And you'll know it's because I want you that way."

She nips at my ear, and my breathing hitches. I've never played in public before, but the idea of being hard all night, knowing it's just for her, is nearly too much to handle. I can already tell tonight is going to be agony, my cock hard in my pants and my ass filled with a plug for her.

My cock twitches as she releases me, desperate for more of her touch. I crash back into the bed, relieved to have her hands off me temporarily and yet already craving for her to touch me again.

"Get dressed and kneel by the vanity for me," she says softly. She takes me by the hand and gently guides me so I'm sitting upright.

The plug shifts in my ass as I move, and a thrill rolls through my body. I'll never get over how good it feels to be filled.

I'm already craving the moment when my mistress finally thrusts into me. I want to feel the smooth leather of her harness and the cool metal of the buckles holding everything in place. I want to be used, to be owned by her in that moment when she drives her cock deep into me. I want her to lay waste to my body and leave me wrung out and boneless.

My need for her grows, and with each step she takes away from me, all I can do is stare.

She slips on a pink velvet dress over her lingerie, which hugs her curves and cowls along her bodice to expose just enough of her breasts. I could watch her forever like this, vulnerable as she gets dressed in finery that's nothing compared to her natural figure.

Her body is on full display in the dress, and every curve is fully exposed. I love how she lets her breasts spill out from the top of the dress and how her belly and thighs show through the ruching. She's fearless, so unafraid of being completely herself.

I envy the comfort and confidence she always has in herself.

Then, she turns back to me, where I still sit on the edge of the bed and takes a few short strides into my space. Suddenly, the collar I wear goes tight around my neck as she pulls up on the leash to get my attention.

"Move, dog," she snaps before tossing the leash back in my face.

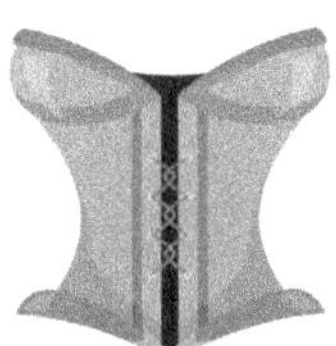

Mistress

We're sitting close in the car, barely a breath between us, and I love the feel of how my soft curves press into his hard physique. Standing, even in heels, my pet towers over me, but it never makes me feel small. I feel delicate, treasured, nestled into his side with my head resting on his hard chest.

The electricity throbbing between our bodies magnifies with each second. I feel each slight movement he makes while trying to adjust to the feeling of a plug in his ass and a ring around his cock. Though we discarded his physical collar and leash in the room before we left, the toys keeping my pet occupied are my display of ownership tonight. Seeing him squirm brings a smile to my face. He is trying, at least.

He better behave.

"Are you looking forward to dinner, pet?" I ask as I reach over to tease and stroke his already hard cock through his dress pants.

"Yes," he pants out, burying his face into my curls. "Fuck. Babe. What are you doing to me?"

I withdraw my touch and lean back to look him in the eye. "What did you just call me?"

His soft eyes, crinkled edges and all widen at the censure in my voice. There's a tenseness to his strong jaw, which he had previously lacking, and his brow furrows when he realizes his mistake.

"Fuck. Sorry. Mistress," he says, dropping his face into my shoulder. "It's just . . . so much. Your touch . . ."

His honeyed words spread warmth through me, and while I appreciate flattery, this is not the time for it.

"That's not what I asked, pet." My nails dig into his thigh, and he lets out a hiss of pain. "What. Did. You call me."

"Babe. I called you babe," he pants out.

Oh, he is in so much trouble when we get back to the hotel. Releasing his thigh, I bring my hand up to trace a trail up and down his neck before letting my fingers settle into the short hair at the base. He melts a little as I grasp slightly at his root, but I don't let him lose himself to the feeling.

I pull tight on his hair, forcing his head back. "Your disobedience today is unparalleled." My lips go to his ear, where I trace my lips over the curves there. "I mean, really, pet, at this rate, how do you expect this night to end?"

"Do you want me to be a brat, Mistress?" he asks, turning his blown-out gaze to me ever so slightly from within my grasp.

"Do you want me to slap you? I have a feeling that's in your future if you act up." I grin and release my grip on his hair, taking him by the chin so he faces me fully.

Even with him looking down at me, I feel empowered. His eyes are glassy with want, and his evident desire makes my pussy throb.

Since the beginning, my pet has possessed this power over me. It's not based on control but rather a strong sense of belonging, which I freely give in to. He can look at me in a way that makes me feel like I could conquer the world if I wanted to. His pure belief in me is addicting, and it's part of what draws me to him. His desire and need for me keep me coming back.

"Yes." His eyes sparkle before dying out when he sees my frown. "No. Please. No. I'm sorry. I want to be good, Mistress. Let me be good."

His breathing is shallow, but he allows me to hold him in place between my fingers. With my free hand, I let myself trace up and down the buttons of his dress shirt, smoothing my hand along his pec. His body is a masterpiece, slender, muscular, and clearly hard-won.

"You know you'll be punished again for that, right?" I ask.

"Yes, Mistress. Whatever I deserve. Anything."

I let my lips hover a whisper away from his own. His eyes flick about my face, taking in everything and nothing all at once. Stars have disappeared from his eyes, and now all I see is the reflection of my brilliance.

Craving his nearness, I unbuckle myself and swing my legs to straddle his own. The position puts my pussy precariously close to his rigid cock. I settle myself right on his length, letting the lace of my underwear press into the light wool of his dress pants and add friction to where I already need him.

But patience is my mistress tonight, and the enduring is rewarded when she's in control.

"Oh, pet. Don't give your mistress such free rein. I might take you seriously," I whisper, giving him a light peck on the lips as his hands wrap around my waist, securing me in place as the car rolls to a stop.

Backing away, I take him in. He's an Adonis, with his tall, built frame and sharp, structured features. He's styled his hair perfectly, tempting me to run my fingers through it just to mess with him a bit. There's a playfulness in the way he's looking at me, laced with pure lust, which makes me melt. And he's all mine.

Bringing my hands up to cup his face, I address him. "You

always have a choice with me. To obey or disobey. Brat or not. Just know I'll respond accordingly."

He nods furiously, shifting under me so his cock presses up into me and makes my eyes flutter shut for a second. "Yes, Mistress. If I need to be punished again, I understand."

"Miss. We're here," the driver interrupts.

"Thank you, Marcus. I'll message you when we are ready to leave," I reply, trying to maintain my cool as I remove myself from my pet's lap and straighten my dress that's ridden up on my hips.

Pet catches on quickly and opens the door to let us both out, turning back to offer his hand to me when I exit the vehicle. His touch sends a chill down my spine, and the heat between us is like that of twin suns. But a longing in his eyes tells me he needs connection, so I loop my arm around his waist, and he cradles me close in his enveloping hold.

Gravity draws us into each other, the magnetic force bringing us closer than may be acceptable in public. It takes every morsel of my restraint, not just to climb him like my personal scratching post, just to get rid of this ache I have for him.

The restaurant is pleasant enough, and my pet does a good job of communicating our needs to the maître d' when we check in at the host stand. As requested, we are led to a quiet table away from families and children and seated with two menus and a booklet of wines.

Pet gazes around the room as I peruse the menu, never even glancing at the options before him, and I recall our first dinner together.

It was yet another Thursday evening before he departed for his home base the next day. The stress of the week had his whole body tense as he sat there trying to read the menu. We sat in silence the entire time until the waiter approached us. Even then, though, he froze when it came time to order, as though every thought had run from his mind. In the very second, he'd paled like a ghost. He'd looked up at me, desperately asking me to intervene and take away whatever fear had risen in him.

It was the first time I recognized him as mine.

"I'm getting the steak," I say, drawing myself away from the memory. "And you?"

"Whatever you desire, Mistress," he says with a small smile.

There's a boldness to his voice, which was lacking earlier in the hotel lobby. Pride swells in my chest at his willingness to let go, to trust.

"I've never done this before," he continues, his leg bouncing up and down.

The rounded booth allows us to sit close together, and I take advantage of this by shifting closer to him.

"Hmm?" I purr, facing him fully.

He goes to place his hand on my thigh but pulls back when he finds it exposed, my dress too short to cover much with all of my curves. He's done this before in large groups, reaching for me like I'm the only thing keeping him grounded in place. So I guide his hand back to rest on the bare skin. His touch there nearly makes me groan when he lightly caresses the inside of my thigh. The back-and-forth movement of his fingertips on my skin, a nervous tick of his I love, is hypnotizing, and it's ramping up my lust.

"Umm . . ." He swallows as I slide my hand up his thigh, near his cock. "Never . . . played . . . like this. Before. In . . . public."

This is all part of why I wanted to bring him here like this. It's one thing to be vulnerable to someone in private, to hand yourself over to them completely in a room with only you and your partners present. The simplicity of a quiet play space with someone eases the part of your mind which keeps you tense. It frees you to submit or rebel against your Domme. It gives you the chance to fully let go.

But playing in public? Even when it's done discreetly, like wearing a collar in a crowded room with others around, it keeps you on edge and increases your awareness of your connection with another person.

"And?" I prompt.

Going to dinner like this means spending an entire hour or more of mental foreplay with my pet, and I'm thrilled.

"It feels different." The slight shudder he lets out is satisfying.

A light glisten shines on his forehead and his eyes frantically scan the room, expecting to be caught. The anticipation and unknowns are part of the fun of playing like this. I control much of the situation, but there is always the possibility of something happening and someone learning our secret.

"Thrilling, isn't it?" I murmur into his ear, letting myself nip at the outer curve. "Knowing you have a naughty secret, you're hiding. That full feeling pressing into your ass, reminding me who you belong to. Your cock strangled by the ring I've put you in."

Pet's whole body freezes, his grip on my thigh tightening as he turns to me with wide eyes and a dropped jaw.

I love seeing him like this and know what he's feeling right now. He's lost to the sensations overwhelming his body. The external stimulus of the restaurant and all its patrons makes something simple, like schooling your expressions, a major feat.

"You'll adjust soon enough . . . but I do enjoy watching you squirm," I say, patting his cock lightly before withdrawing to my own space, though making sure to stay close enough to be a comfort to him.

I keep my hand tantalizingly close to his hard cock, and I'm able to gently trace his shaft with my pinky while I place both our orders with the waiter.

Our appetizers come and go with little conversation between us other than pleasantries. Then, when the waiter leaves with our plates, my deep curiosity, pulled forth by a bit of my masochism, has a particular question on my tongue.

I'm desperate to ask, but I know I shouldn't push him like this, not now. It's never a good idea to talk through difficult topics while in the midst of play, but I need to know. Especially before tonight goes any further.

He looks so sweet, and I wonder what could have prompted such a good-natured man to abandon me the way he did. There must be a good reason, but I can't fathom what it might be. Pet appears oblivious to my inner conflict. His focus is entirely engrossed in the napkin he's fiddling with, and when, under my scrutiny, he glances in my direction, I can't hold myself back any longer.

I reach over to take his hand in mine, intertwining our fingers. His full attention turns to me, and my gaze connects with his own silver stare.

"At some point, you're going to need to explain your disappearance," I say softly, giving his hand a light squeeze.

When he bites his lip and breaks eye contact with me, my heart bottoms out. He's hiding from me, and it doesn't matter if it's himself or something else. We've had countless conversations about how necessary open communication and honesty are. Outright, it was something the two of us could quickly agree upon in those early days.

So, what happened to the man who so readily jumped to give me his world?

"I've asked you for a lot this evening." I pause, hoping his focus will return to me . . . .It doesn't. "We need to decide if we want this thing between us to continue, and I can't do that without a full picture of what's happening."

Pet's shoulders crumple, closing his body off to me, but I push on. "I can't move forward without knowing why you left me alone like that."

Something stirs in him, and his posture straightens. It's like he's now able to address me directly. "But you aren't alone. You have Durante."

"Yes, I will always have my sir. But alone is different than lonely." Something about the glimmer of despair in his eyes makes me reconsider this conversation for a second. "But you were both, weren't you?"

His squirming is no longer due to my physical control over his body. Instead, the tight one-handed grip on his napkin and the way he bounces his knee tells me it's something more.

"Tell me." I pause, knowing he needs more from me than just my request. "Please, baby."

Jaw dropped, pet faces me, and I can see how he's processing behind his eyes.

The fidgeting doesn't stop, but he slows his movements. I take a deep breath in and out, counting the entire time, and eventually, his inhales and exhales match mine. Tension slowly leaches from his body as we breathe together.

"You know I was getting divorced?" he says quietly.

"Was?" I ask, knowing he won't choose his words without purpose.

A slight smirk sneaks onto his lips. "Yeah, it was. It's over now."

"That's wonderful!" I start cheerfully, but then his face falls once more.

"It . . . It wasn't . . . good," he mutters.

"Never is, pet."

I run my thumb back and forth over the back of his hand as he gathers himself.

"No. It was . . . brutal. Sh-she . . ." His voice quivers like I've never heard before. "Melanie found out about us."

My eyebrows rise at the implication. Without saying the words, I already know she used our relationship to manipulate and sabotage my darling pet.

"She called me all these nasty things: vile, immoral, perverted, depraved, a monster, and a degenerate. And I handled her petty hits when it was just directed at me. But she found out about you .

. . .I couldn't . . . I wouldn't do that to you. You don't deserve to be dragged into my mess."

I sit back against the bench seating, still not letting go of his hand. "So instead of talking to me, you chose to vanish. Why?"

His questioning response is immediate. "Because of all those things. I didn't want . . ."

"No. You made a choice. You didn't just disappear. You fled. Instead of running to me for support, you ran away. Why?" Durante is the licensed therapist, but years of being with him has taught me a thing or two about leading someone to their realizations. "And if you felt that way about her words, how do you feel about mine? When I named you mutt? Or told you you're worthless?"

His brow furrows as he battles through my prompt.

Nothing between us will ever work if he's uncomfortable sharing with me. He's given me his body and mind, but his heart feels so far away. That's what I'm asking him for, his most vulnerable self. I want to know *him* better than he knows himself. It's the only way I can protect him from the cruelties of the world.

I'm surprised by his response, nonetheless. "I need it in a way I've never known before. With you, it feels like finally being seen."

"I'll always see you, pet," I say as my hand squeezes his tighter, and he returns the feeling to the point where I worry he may crush my hand. He's clinging to me, and I couldn't be more honored.

"Can we . . . be done?" He pauses. "For now, at least. I don't want to focus on the past right now."

"You want to look to the future with me?" He nods, and my heart swells. "Yeah, we can close this matter tonight," I smile.

The rest of dinner is wonderful, some of the tension which hovered between us now dissipated. But our meal is still not quite as delicious as every reaction from my pet throughout it. His struggle to sit still and maintain eye contact has me heated and tingling with anticipation.

I love touching and teasing him as we chat about mundane things like media and work. He's only able to pick at most of his food, and it brings me great pleasure to help him. There's something so sensual about lifting a fork to his mouth and having him wrap his lips around the utensil to eat. It conjures images of his lips wrapped around my breast, my cunt, and my cock.

At the end of my second cocktail and our dessert, I turn to him fully. "How are you feeling, pet?" I say, leaning into his ear while letting the back of my hand fully caress his cock. "Are you needy for me yet? Ready to go? Or should I make you sit with me for a coffee and biscotti?"

Besides our light conversation, he's been mostly quiet, but the pathetic whimper he lets out at my threat to elongate the evening sends a tingling sensation through every nerve in my body. The reaction lights me up with a broad smile. I can see the war within him to agree to my request, and while battling the neediness, I'm guessing he's suffering.

"Yes. Please, Mistress." His whispered reply doesn't even come as a shock. "Can we go back now? You have my cock aching. I want to be inside you, but I need you inside me more."

"Patience, pet," I purr while turning my hand to grasp his dick and squeeze harshly.

He hisses a breath and moans, then glances around the room with a red flush on his cheeks.

"Excuse me," I say to the waiter as they pass. "Could we get the check?"

"Yes, miss. Of course."

"I'll be in the ladies' room while you pay, pet," I whisper to my companion. "Wait for me in the car. But do *not* touch yourself." His breathing is heavy as I lean in. "You're mine to play with tonight."

I take my time in the restroom, longer than is necessary, to make sure he's writhing for me when I get to the car. My smile breaks free when I open the door, taking in the sight of my pet with his legs spread wide and gripping, white-knuckled, at the seat to keep himself under control. He discarded his suit jacket, loosened his tie and collar, and rolled up the sleeves of his shirt to reveal his forearms.

"Is something wrong, pet?" I raise my brow inquisitively.

"No," he pants out before changing his mind. "Yes. I can feel my dick dripping pre-cum on my leg."

Sliding in next to him, I play my finger over his hand, then, one by one, pry his fingers from where they grasp.

"Mmh. That wet spot on your pants for me, then?" I say, licking up his throat and watching his Adam's apple bob.

"Yes, Mistress." He groans.

Reaching over to stroke him once more through his pants, I give him a tight squeeze before moving up to start unbuckling his belt. "Take it out. Show me, mutt."

His hand snaps out and catches me by the wrist to stop my movement. "I'm afraid." His eyes close at the admission. "My sissy dick isn't like yours."

"True. My cock can fulfill any of your wildest dreams, that's for sure," I say, plucking his hand from around my wrist. "But right now, I've asked you to show me your cock, and I expect you to follow instructions."

He reaches for his belt before hesitating once more, and I scowl when he looks at me. "What will you do to me if I'm too scared to show you?"

"Then, I'm definitely picking up a flogger tonight so I can beat your ass red," I say, my words clipped and my breathing erratic.

I want him exposed to me. The foreplay at dinner has built up my desire into a blazing fire. The inertia of our time in our secluded corner of the restaurant is sending me tumbling toward a cliff of bliss I don't want to escape. But I try to remember this is just as much about him as it is my pleasure.

My emotions have been a pendulum since he first stepped out

of the elevator this evening. Every moment with him has pushed me closer to my limit, but each infraction is met with another reminder of why I yearn for him. His brazenness of the night starkly contrasts with the angelic memory I've built of him.

I shouldn't compare the two. I know I've inflated him in my mind after all this time, but he's turned into a terror before my eyes. So, I keep trying to remind myself he's not perfect.

And sometimes, good boys misbehave.

My response is slow. "If I have to punish you for this little act of rebellion, I'm withholding other things. You understand that, right?"

"Yes. I understand."

It was so simple with Lily, and I can't help but compare the two. She was a natural submissive, every part of her longing to obey and listen. She was so perfect for a long time. Her only mistake was thinking I only wanted her in the bedroom and not in my life. I wanted my kitten at my feet but also at my side.

Pet, on the other hand, doesn't seem to understand anything, which makes me question his place in my life.

My pet takes his time freeing himself from the confines of his clothing, but then his cock springs into action. "Shit. My sissy dick is dripping. I can't . . . I want . . ."

"What you want doesn't matter," I say.

He's hot and pulsing in my hand. My mouth waters, and I want to take him deep down my throat, but I stop myself.

I have better games to play.

"Oh, pet. You're already leaking for me," I say, gathering up his pre-cum on my fingers and positioning them at his mouth. "Come now, taste for Mistress."

He looks at me, a little startled. We have discussed consuming bodily fluids, and while some are off the table, he gave consent to eating his cum. But the sudden suggestion seems to have caught him off guard.

Slowly, he leans forward and opens his mouth for me. I push forward, forcing him to taste the saltiness of himself to the back of his throat. I let him gag slightly for a second before withdrawing, but before my fingers are free, his eyes fall shut, and his mouth closes around them.

"Good job, pet. Such good practice for when you suck my cock," I say as his tongue runs along the pads of my fingers. I thrust them in and out as he licks and sucks them clean, and it makes my pussy throb. "That's the first instruction you've followed successfully tonight. Don't think it will get you out of your punishment, though."

"I know. I was bad. I'm sorry," he says when I finally pull my fingers from his mouth.

"You will be, pet. Your ass is going to be so red, you'll feel it all day tomorrow. A nice reminder of your disobedience today."

I drag my fingers over his lips, and he shudders.

I can't wait to get a flogger in my hand to make his body sing with pain and pleasure. To work him up with sensations all over his skin and light strokes on his ass until he's begging for the pain I am capable of bestowing. I want to leave a handprint on his ass and let it blend into the rest of the red I'll leave on his body by the end of the night.

"I think, though, if you take your punishment well, I may yet fuck you tonight. Would you like that, pet?"

My pussy throbs as I picture myself putting on my harness and affixing one of the dildos he selected in place. I want him to shiver and squirm when I apply lube to his puckered hole and finger him there. Then, I'll take my cock and tease him with it until the only word on his lips is, *please.*

"Yes, Mistress. I want it so much." He groans, bucking his hips up.

"I think I'd like to stare at your raw ass while I fuck you." Another picture comes to me in memory of one of his earlier requests. "And maybe I can stuff another cock down your throat while I pound into your pathetic little hole."

His cock gives a jerk at my suggestion. "I'll shove the cock in my mouth if you tell me what to do."

I take his face into both of my hands, and his gaze turns absolutely molten with heat and desire. "Yes, you'd like that, wouldn't you, you worthless mutt?" I give him a few pats on the cheek before finishing with a light slap to his face.

Impact play has always been part of our agreement, but using it as a tool for humiliation is new for both of us. His eyes sparkle with a threat, which makes my breath catch.

He's testing me, seeing how far I will be pushed until I snap. Our time apart scarred my pet in ways I can't begin to imagine. His hurt is his only guiding light, a direction which should be coming from me.

I've been acting under the presumption that everything could easily revert to the way things were before, that he is coming back into my life as the same good boy he was.

But he's not, and he can't be.

I clench my jaw, knowing I've both failed him and myself. I'm not the woman, the Domme he needs. Sir always tells me anger has its place. It exists in our hearts and heads for a reason. It's a good motivator and an indicator of extreme discomfort or danger.

Right now, my anger needs to be my tool.

He wants to rebel and fight me at every turn. His taut body says he's ready to fight, but the sadness in his eyes says he wants to give in more. It's my job, my honor, to get him there.

A spark in my chest has me leaning in. "You want to do as you're told. I know you do."

"Please, Mistress. I'm so close. Will you let me come in my face?" he pleads.

"Not yet, pet. But *if* I let you cum tonight, you're going to clean up every last drop. Even if I have to swipe it up with my fingers and shove it down your throat myself." I release him and straighten myself where I sit, turning my attention to the road and the hotel that approaches, but my pet doesn't seem to notice yet.

"I understand," he replies meekly, completely focused on my face. Out of my periphery, I can see him work up the courage to tell me what he wants. "I want you to break me."

My heart is heavy at the admission, the truth of the statement.

"If you're good, I will." I sigh.

"What else are you going to do to me?" he asks.

The simplicity of the question almost sends me into a spiral with all the things I want to do to his body, but I hold myself back from getting lost in the fantasies.

We have time.

"You'll find out soon enough, pet," I reply before tapping his dick lightly with the back of my hand, not even looking in his direction. "Put it away. I don't want you traumatizing the valet."

5

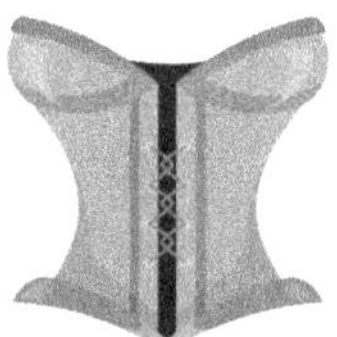

Mistress

My whole focus has shifted to be solely on him, my pet. He's done better since I plugged him. His punishment settled him slightly, but he is fidgeting where he stands just inside the door to the suite. His shoulders are hunched forward, and he's refusing to look me in the eye.

Unacceptable.

"Strip," I command as I cross toward my bag of goodies, turning my back to him.

The bag sits on the vanity stool, and I admire my pet as he strips in the reflection of the mirror before me. There's a nervous energy about him, but the farther he follows me into the room, the more his confidence returns.

Each piece of his clothing coming off is like another layer of his mask he sheds. His dress shirt exposes the white of his under-shirt just as much as it exposes his vulnerability. When he unbuttons and drops his pants, some of his cockiness falls away. The whole process is mesmerizing, but I manage to pull my attention back to the items laid on the vanity stool before me.

When I look back into the mirror, he fixates on me with intense heat in his eyes. His gaze is like the center of his universe. Sometimes, when he thinks I'm not looking, I see this longing in his expression. It reflects my own desire to stay within his presence, and the feeling haunts me.

After putting the bag to the side and settling into the seat, I let myself ogle him as I slid the zipper at the back of my dress down. The soft velvet straps fell off my shoulders, revealing my light-pink, lacy lingerie set.

He jumps back into action, stripping off his final articles of clothing. But just as he knows I prefer, he takes each piece and folds it neatly before placing it on the dresser. It's cute, though, how he keeps his socks on.

His fully naked reflection has me turning around to take him in, but my eyes widen when I get to his firm chest. There, right over his heart, is a tattoo that was previously not there.

I stand and move. My hand is outstretched to hover just above it when I'm before him.

"When did . . . ?" I whisper, looking up at him wide-eyed.

"A few weeks ago. Do you like it?" he says hopefully.

The softness in his rich rumble makes me think my opinion suddenly means the world to him.

But I have to know, so I ask. "Does it matter if I do?"

"Yes," he says in a low voice as he encompasses my small outstretched hand in his own massive ones. "Very much."

My gaze stays trained on the tattoo, and I take in the eloquent details of the dark side of the moon, the swirls in the sun, and the flares that billow outward. The star's path is faint among the details, almost like it's losing its orbit before it returns. But it hugs close to the light and the darkness of the eclipse.

"What does it mean?" I ask, feigning naïveté.

"You know what it means." His lips form a small frown, and his brows furrow.

"Yes. I do," I soothe, looking him in the eye. "And you need to say it out loud."

Silence drags on, and he opens and closes his mouth several times before working up the courage to actually speak. "You're my sun. And I'm the star defying gravity to orbit you, just to be in your presence."

Air ceases to exist when I hear his confession. My chest tightens, my throat clogs, and if he weren't clutching my hand so tightly, my hands would be shaking.

"It's too much, S . . ." I stutter.

One of his hands releases me to cover my mouth. The feel of his hand on my lips grounds me as I breathe in and out through my nose. But it also creates a new fantasy in my mind.

I'm imagining him fucking me from above, his hand over my mouth as I cry out in pleasure and pain as his cock drills into me.

But do I really want that?

"No. Please. I don't want to be him. I'm *not* him when I'm with you. I want to be your pet, your mutt, your plaything. Anything to keep me close to you." He withdraws his hand and takes a step closer to me, lowering his forehead to rest on my own despite his towering stature. "I missed you, and I was too scared to admit it. Too scared to reach out to you. But I didn't just hurt you. I was punishing myself when I held back. Please, Mistress. Please."

I can't hold myself back any longer. I reach up with both hands to grab his face and pull him down for a kiss. His lips are warm, and he melts into me, his weight pressing me down.

Our bodies fuse together the longer we kiss. His hands stroke down my sides before stopping at the hem of my dress. Lifting his hands, I bring them to the curve between my ass and thigh. He doesn't need any more instructions, not when his other hand follows so deftly. Fingers bite into my flesh, and he swiftly picks me up as my legs automatically wrap around his waist.

All the movement has my dress riding up around my hips, and

my pet gasps as my lace-covered pussy rubs against his throbbing cock. It gives him access to my needy core, and I smirk at his surprise when I grind into his hardness. His hands knead my ass, pushing me closer to him. My hips rock against his cock, turning the barely there heat from friction into a raging inferno.

"No." I gasp when his lips move to my jaw.

Like a good boy, he freezes, and I force myself down from where I cling to him. A shiver rolls through him as I descend, my core grazing against him the whole way down.

"No?" he asks. "What do you mean, no? Don't you want me?"

Every fiber of my being wants him. The inferno of my lust is all-consuming.

"I mean, I refuse to give into lust just because it feels good. If you want me, then you'll be good for me." I raise my eyebrow.

Our whole issue this evening has revolved around the battle between my lust and logic.

"Tell me, my goddess of sun and light . . . Tell me how to serve you." He smirks.

I scoff at the over-the-top praise. "If you want to be good for me, then you'll learn when to stop talking and heel."

His expression goes slack, and his eyes go wide. "What?"

"Down. On your knees," I bite out.

I don't even wait to see if he follows instructions. Instead, I turn and go to the table where I left his leash and collar. I grip tightly to the chain leash, letting the cool metal bite into my skin. When I turn back around, my pet is still standing, but something in my expression must show him my displeasure because he immediately drops to his knees.

"Crawl to me, dog," I command.

There's a flash in his eyes, making me think he wants to disobey, but then he relents. He lowers himself to all fours and takes his first pace forward. His muscles ripple, but his movements are jerky, the plug still buried deep in his ass and the ring tight around his cock that sways awkwardly. The humorous vision has me biting back a smile.

When he's reached my feet, he raises himself back to his knees, but I stop him with my heel. I let the sole of my shoe press into his shoulder slightly, but when he pushes up against me, I give in to my desire and dig my heel into the flesh. With most of my weight on his shoulder, his arm collapses beneath him, and he's nearly where I want him.

"Down," I order, and his head turns up to look at me, the rebellion shining in his eyes, spiking my frustration.

"Down, boy," I snarl. "And kiss your mistress's feet."

I release him from beneath my heel and bring the pair back together in front of him. He looks back and forth between the tips of my metallic hot-pink heels and my face. His narrowed gaze has me thinking he's once again going to disobey, but he surprises me by leaving long, lingering kisses on the tips of my shoes.

"Now sit," I say.

Instructions seem to be permeating his thick skull because he bends up and resumes a kneeling position. The anxious part of me that doubts my ability to provide for this man, support and guide him in the way he needs keeps rearing its head. But seeing him so easily drop to his knees calms the part of me that's been struggling with our changing dynamic.

"Give me your neck," I say.

He lifts his chin as I unbuckle the collar and reach to fasten it around his neck. The leather is firm yet soft in my hand, a perfect symbol of my method of claiming him. When I fasten it around his neck, I choose a hole tighter than before, sliding two fingers inside the band, where I can feel his pulse thrumming.

Turning away, I let my velvet dress fall from my body, revealing all of my lingerie to him. A glance up into the mirror reveals his erect cock. He's ready for me physically, but my doubt returns. Fear I'm not what he needs, that I can't handle him.

He's not used to all this, being brand new to the lifestyle and dynamics. I'm realizing our beginning seemed simple because of what he didn't know about his preferences. He followed my lead so well at first, but now I see he is far more of a brat than I realized.

As though he can hear my thoughts, he raises his hand to touch me, but I whip around to face him and push down on his wrist forcefully.

"I said heel." He drops his eyes, and something snaps in me. "When you heel for me, you will be on your knees at my side and you do not move from your position. You will wait patiently for your next instruction. And your eyes will remain on me." I run my fingers through his soft curls before tugging tightly on his roots. "And, pet? When you heel . . . you don't speak."

His teeth dig into his bottom lip, and he nods.

I turn back to the vanity mirror and take a deep breath before reaching for my cotton pads and makeup remover. My nightly cleansing ritual is a balm to the hurt of the day. My whole body relaxes as I take off the mask I wear in public and step into a more centered version of myself.

Pulling up my hair into a high ponytail, I spot my pet biting his tongue out of the corner of my eye, and I slow my movements just to see how long it takes before his impulse to speak wins.

It's not long.

"Why are you taking off your makeup?" he blurts out.

I take a deep breath before turning to him. "Well, for one, I fully plan on collapsing into bed tonight when I'm finished with you."

A smile graces his face, warming the part of my heart which is quickly growing cold.

"And two?" he asks.

I exhale deeply, turning my voice soft. "This dynamic requires good communication, but more importantly, vulnerability. This is play, but I'm not playing games with you, pet," I say, taking hold of his chin to make him look me in the eye. "We are Mistress and pet, but we are still wholly ourselves. I want you to see me as I am, just as I see you for who you are."

Tears form in the corners of his eyes while his Adam's apple bobs as he gulps down a choked breath. The emotion seems to overwhelm him and his gaze drops away from me and down to the ground.

"Pet." My tone has turned to stone. "Look. At. Me."

I hate the abrupt changes in my mood and how he tests my patience and my control. I don't like being an angry person, but the constant pushback from him has my frustration gathering to a peak of white-hot anger. There's no place for anger in a dynamic. Not a healthy one, at least.

When he looks back at me, he expresses trepidation, which causes me to suppress my frustration and opt for a calm voice. "Your vulnerability is not a weakness. It's a gift, as is your submission."

"I don't understand," he whispers.

"I know, but you will . . ." I pause. "You have no reason to fear me. I would never harm you. You know that, right? I mean . . . maybe cause temporary hurt, but never harm. Do you understand?"

The time he takes to deeply consider my words has my chest tightening. The conflict I've felt all day, the doubt I've had about our relationship, or rather what we could be together, comes back in full force.

"Yes," he replies, calming all of my darker thoughts.

"And you want . . ." I pause. "Tonight, you're consenting to . . . ?"

I let the words linger, but he doesn't fill in the blank I've left open.

Realizing he's, for once, obeying my command to heel, I say, "Speak, pup."

A cocky smirk appears on his lips as he responds. "Whatever you deem appropriate. Anything for you."

His expression is entirely open, and a chill runs down my spine as want gathers in my body. The images of him spread out for me, unable to move while I play with his body, play across my mind.

He'd be so helpless and so *mine*.

"You keep saying that. I think we may just need to test your theory." My smile is devious. "Open."

I grip his face tightly in my hand, turning his face to meet my own and pressing down on his cheeks. He opens his mouth in response, tilting his head back at the perfect angle for me to spit into his mouth.

"Pitiful. Even for a mangy dog." I sneer as he swallows.

Pet's response to the insult only encourages me. The deeper we explore this component of our dynamic, the more responsive he becomes. Though his outward reaction shows no explicit expression of it, each step in this new direction has him suppressing his enjoyment. His eyes glitter with every cruel word I hurl at him and every shameful action I put him through.

There's fulfillment on both sides, though. Degradation has never really been my thing, or so I thought. But the past hours with my pet have made me realize the humiliation is more gratifying than I realized. There's a satisfaction in having a partner who's pliable and open to this kind of play.

This is just taking it a step further.

A firm shove to his shoulders has him falling back, landing on his hands in an awkward bent position. This time, though, he stays like a good boy.

Rising from my seat on the vanity, I step to straddle his chest and raise one stiletto. I place it on his shoulder, and he hisses as the heel bites into the tender skin near his collarbone.

"I think we should start with you getting your ass beaten with the plug-in. How does that sound, mutt? Should I beat you until you finally learn your lesson? Until you know how to be a good boy and obey? Because you haven't been doing very well so far."

A swift knock to his chest with the ball of my foot has him collapsing to the floor.

I turn around, taking in the array of instruments available. Satisfaction swells at the thought of all the pain and pleasure I'll conjure tonight. Plans form as I take in the floggers, paddles, wands, and more.

"Are you ready for your punishment, pet?" I ask over my shoulder but don't wait for his response. "Up against the wall. Spread your legs for me."

I try to ignore the flex and pull of my pet's taut muscles as he climbs up from the floor, but the room's lighting only seems to accentuate each perfectly toned part of him.

To hide my blush, I return to studying the array of instruments laid out for me. My hands trace over the various impact play tools, each with its own purpose to cause a particular sensation.

Settling on one of the floggers, I pick it up to test the feel and weight in my hand. It's lighter than I prefer, and I can't help but long for my collection of instruments from my friend, Phoenix.

These toys chosen by my pet will do, but there's nothing like something personalized for you. These will be christened for my pet. He chose his own punishment tonight and will pay the price we agreed upon.

"Hands on the wall, legs spread apart," I command.

Pet scrambles to obey, positioning himself against the wall as I've asked. The state puts his slim form on full display. He's a vision in his nakedness, every muscle under his pale skin show-cased by the way he's angled.

My slow steps bring me to his side, and my hand runs up and

down his back, finally resting at the base of his spine. "If I recall correctly, your yes/ no/ maybe list denoted you've never been flogged before, correct? But it's of high interest to you, right?"

He nods enthusiastically.

"Use your words, pet," I prompt.

"Yes, Mistress. I would very much like to experience flogging." His voice is sure and strong.

There's no doubt in my mind he's being truthful. The brightness in his eyes tells me as much, and my heartbeat skips at his enthusiasm.

My hand slides down to rest on his ass, and I squeeze the tight muscle before giving him a light smack on his ass cheek. "Good."

I can't help but see the smile forming on my face as I move behind him, and I'm grateful he can't see my delight. It would make him far too smug.

Delivering punishment is as much of a pleasure and release for me as receiving it in kind. Still, there's nothing quite like holding a weighted flogger in your hand, striking it against your partners over and over while watching the reddened evidence of your work form on their skin.

"I'm going to start soft to get you used to the sensation, and I'll work my way up. But unless you use your safeword, unless you safe-out, I'm not holding back when I reach your threshold," I explain, warming up my wrists and shoulders in preparation for what I feel will be an extensive session.

Flogger in hand, the lightest and longest of the bunch, I twirl it by the handle to get a feel for its movement. The first swipe through the air has the leather moving nimbly with a light swoosh, but I want to test its limits, just as I'll test my pet.

The leather falls swoop high on my twirl, and I forcefully bring them down. But before the next downstroke completes its path through empty air, I hold my left forearm out before me. The impact is mild against my delicate skin, and I repeat the process until I'm comfortable with the various sensations it can produce.

Testing the limits of toys on myself to gauge their capabilities is never a replacement for reading body language and listening to a sub's reactions. Still, thankfully, my own experience as a sub informs my ability to wield instruments like a flogger with ease.

Out of the corner of my eye, I watch my pet, and with each swirl of the flogger, he tenses. Every loud thwack of the falls causes him to jerk, thinking he's next. The mental torment is surely ramping up his fear and desire, adrenaline coursing through both our bodies.

As I begin to play with him, I slowly run the tendrils of the flogger up his legs and back. Each stroke along his body is another key to his undoing. Muscles unclench, smoothing out before my eyes as he relaxes into the trickle of leather on his skin. Gradually, he gives himself over, inch by inch, to the soothing sensation I bestow upon him.

Watching him like this, totally trusting despite knowing what's coming for him, unlocks the tension that's held my body captive. His faith further thaws my fears of inadequacy. There's an innocence that comes with not knowing what to expect, but there's also an electric energy that exists in the same space.

Each play session I have with a hilt in my hand gives me a sense of calm and confidence. Here, I know who I am and what I'm doing. I'm a mistress of pleasure and pain, comfort and consequence.

Pet finally relaxes in his stance when I decide to change it up and lightly swing the falls between his legs to just kiss his balls, still caught in the noose of his ring. His heels lift off the ground, and he squeaks in surprise, but he doesn't object. Not that he would, as cock and ball torture, CBT, is right up his alley and on his list.

"You like that, pet?" I ask, swinging between his legs once more.

He groans deeply. "Yes, Mistress. A lot."

"Poor pet," I say, halting my movements. "That was the exact wrong thing to say."

I hide my delight behind a smirk, knowing how much trouble we could both get into if he keeps this up. His enjoyment of how I tease him only strokes my ego as I play.

I adjust my grip on the hilt, shifting it so my palm rests closer to the butt of the handle, and I have more flexibility in my wrist.

Bringing the tresses up, I let my wrist flick the instrument down and across pet's ass before following through across my body. I repeat the action, backhanded this time, and start to fall into a rhythm with each figure eight I make.

I let gravity do the work, and soon, my pet is squirming. With impatience or anticipation, it doesn't matter. Accelerating my wrist, I let the tails fly in a vertical movement, like a fencing moulinet, before adding force on its final downward stroke, which makes my pet cry out.

I switch between rhythmic figures and harsh lashes on his shoulders, ribcage, and backside, admiring the reddening skin with each movement I make. I let myself get lost in the ebbs and flows of the pattern, changing it up when I recognize my pet is anticipating too much.

His breathing has turned from heavy to gasping, and I pause to approach him.

"How are you feeling, mutt?" I ask, checking in and massaging his ass with my free hand.

Hands still on the wall, he turns his face to meet mine. "Good, Mistress."

"And your color?"

Doubt creeps in as I consider for a second how it will feel if he says anything other than green. Does it mean I'm a failure of a Domme? Have I misled him or caused him harm? He's taken so much tonight that I wouldn't mind stopping at all. But if our dynamic is to succeed, I need us to be on the same page so that we can meet each other's needs.

He takes a few deep breaths as I rub his back and ass to hopefully relieve some of the hurt with pressure.

"Green, Mistress," he says, looking me straight in the eye, and I believe him.

Letting him catch his breath, I go to my bag and grab one of the water bottles inside. I crack the lid as I walk back to him but pull back when he reaches out to take it from me.

"Let me," I say, holding the bottle to his lips as he takes a few solid gulps. "Good pet."

When he finishes, I down the rest and place the empty bottle in the trash can. Pet is still in the same position when I turn around, hands on the wall and legs spread apart.

But between his legs is a beautiful sight.

His cock, still snug in its ring, is leaking onto the floor. There's a string of pre-cum hanging from his tip, and something about the vision makes my mouth water.

There's nothing like a bit of torment to make a man's cock weep.

"I'm going to give you a final ten strokes on each side, okay?" I tell him, switching and twirling the flogger in my nondominant hand to minimize the potential damage I could cause.

"Yes, Mistress," he replies.

I check in again, needing him to reassure me just as much as himself. "Color, pet."

"Green, Mistress," he replies immediately.

"Good." I smile broadly and bring down the flogger's tails hard against his left cheek.

"Fuck me," he cries out, but I don't relent.

For his first time, I only deliver five on each side, though my sir would say I'm half-assing it.

I'm fully focused on controlling my aim and evening the strikes on his body, trying my best not to hit in the same spot too often. I almost don't hear his whisper. "I can't stand anymore."

Fuck.

Immediately, I stop and toss the flogger on the couch behind me. I don't even bother looking to see where it lands before I'm moving to take him in my arms. His bare torso is hot from my lashings when I wrap myself around him, and I bury my face into his spine.

His trembling has concern constricting my chest, and the confidence that built me up and reassured my capability as a Domme while I played with him dissipates. My earlier guilt and doubt come crashing back as I cling to him.

"That's alright, pet," I say, failure stealing my breath. "You did so well for me. We can stop."

"No. I don't want to stop. Please." He groans, but his body has other ideas when his knees buckle, and he falls back into my arms.

"Oh!" I gasp out.

I tighten my grip around him and walk myself backward, lowering us both down gently to the floor. His legs stretch out before him, but he flinches when his reddened skin makes contact with the textured carpet. Overwhelmed by the need to comfort and soothe my pet, I finish setting him down before moving to straddle him from behind. His whole body sags into mine, and I revel in his heat, how his bare skin feels penetrating through the lace of my lingerie.

"I'm so sorry. I should have noticed sooner," I say, placing kisses up and down his spine where I can reach.

I let my hands roam all over his body, his chest and thighs and back, anywhere I can touch. I'm desperate to make sure he's okay, knowing all the while it's only to assuage my guilt.

"No. Don't apologize," he says when he's caught his breath. "I wanted to take it. I wanted to take more. It was . . . freeing."

The way his body relaxes at the admission lightens some of the weight on my chest, but I'm still recovering from my earlier spike of panic.

I think back to how his body shook as I flogged him, how I took enjoyment from the stress I put him through. Pride overwhelmed me as he took each lashing, and the euphoria blinded me when he neared his limits.

I admit, "But I shouldn't push you past your physical limits. I don't want to harm you."

His next gasp for breath isn't one from breathlessness but from emotion. Turning him in my hold, I cling to him like a monkey to a tree as tears fall from his reddened eyes.

"Shhh. Sweet pet. I'm so sorry," I say, a regretful sorrow welling in my chest. "I pushed you too far. That's my fault. You did so good. You took your punishment so well. Let's take a break, okay?"

He shakes his head as he buries it into my shoulder and croaks out, "No. More. I want more."

Damp tears on my shoulder cloud my sanity, and the need to fix things becomes too much, but my pet is asking me for something. I know from experience that pain can be as much of an emotional release as it is sexual, and the bit of knowledge reassures me a little as I debate, giving in to his request.

"Give me a color," I say softly, bringing his chin up to look at me.

"Green." He sighs as his gaze connects with mine.

"Are you lying to me?" I ask, squeezing his chin between my fingers.

"No, Mistress. Green. I want more. I deserve more, worse. Use me until I'm fully yours. Let me lose myself to you." I consider his words, and my heart swells a bit. "Please. I'm not worthy of you.

Break me, please. I want to fall apart for you and reform into something better . . . for you," he begs.

I search his eyes, looking for any hint of hesitation or unease. And while I find some discomfort, likely from the physical beating he just took, everything in his expression tells me he, too, is consumed by a desperate need for me, just as I am for him. "On the bed," I command.

6

———

Pet

Part of me wants to stay in her hold like this, to just lie in her arms as she presses kisses to the curve of my neck and spine. The heat of her little body against my own makes me melt, but I drag myself from within her warmth and push up to stand.

Turning around to face her, where she's still straddled open on the floor like a doll, I take in the concern on her face.

"I'm okay," I promise, smirking and holding out a hand to help her up.

I watch her as she runs through everything in her mind before she takes my hand. I pull hard, making her fly up and crash into my body.

After a moment, she mumbles into my chest, "You're sure?"

The vulnerability in her statement warms my heart. I know she cares about me; she wouldn't have agreed to see me again if I didn't hold a place in her heart. But the softness in her voice is all of the validation I need to confirm the heartwarming knowledge.

"Yeah. I'm good," I answer, burying my face in her hair and breathing in her coconut shampoo.

She pulls away, slipping back into play. "Then don't make me repeat myself."

"Yes, ma'am," I say with a little salute and a grin before releasing her and turning toward the bed.

"Brat," she scolds, smacking my ass cheek.

The sting from her hand has me shivering in anticipation. I want her hands back on me, but this time, I want pain again. Her comfort is too much. She's too good for me. There's a part of me that knows this can't last forever, but I can't help but hope it will.

Leaning over and letting my chest rest on the end of the bed, I spread my legs wide in preparation for the next part of my punishment as I pray for her mercy. The plug in my ass shifts, bringing about a whole new sensation as it presses into me at a new angle. All the while, the ring around my shaft and balls grips me tightly enough to have me twitching.

"Are you going to fuck me tonight, Mistress?" I ask, the fullness reminding me of my earlier need for her.

"I'm not sure you deserve it, pet," she says from behind me.

Her hand trails up my back, and her fingers travel into my hair. Her nails scratch at my skull, and I shiver, but a sharp tug at the roots makes me jerk my head up to look at her perfect face.

"You've denied me what I wanted all evening. So why should I reward you with what you've been craving?" she asks, hair falling into her face as she leans into my ear. "Do you deserve my cock or my paddle, mutt?"

She pushes my head forward into the mattress, muffling my response.

"I think you've earned my paddle tonight. You'll have to work much harder next time to earn my dildo in your ass," she taunts.

"This is brand new, you know. I picked it up for myself as a treat," she says, trailing softness up the back of my thighs, cooling some of the heat burning there from my earlier flogging. "I like the contrast of the velvet on one side and the leather and metal brads on the other. So many possible sensations all in one instrument. Brilliant, isn't it?"

She runs the paddle up and down my legs, switching between sides and introducing me to all the paddle's offerings. The texture makes every nerve in my body hyperaware of what is coming.

"But tonight, you're going to become very well acquainted with pain. Aren't you, you miserable mutt?" she says, running her hands over the marks left by the flogger. "You're already off to a good start with all these lashes on your body. Your back is a beautiful display of my markings."

I barely have time to recognize the swoosh of air for what it is before there's a hard thwack on my ass. The paddle's motion stops where it hits, and she applies pressure, thankfully. It alleviates some of the bursting pain the paddle delivers, but it only lessens it instead of changing the sensation, especially with the plug still buried in my ass.

"Fucking hell." I gasp into the mattress while clutching at the sheets.

"That's right. You're not in God's house. You're in mine. Now stay still and beg for my mercy."

The ice in her voice, contrasting the raging heat building in me, makes every hair on my body stand up. There's no malice—I know my mistress would never hurt me—but her tone is a clear threat.

Mistress once again gives me the blessing of easing me into my punishment. She starts by switching between the sides of the paddle. The varying textures leave different sensations on my skin, which have my cock as hard as a diamond on its ring.

Each time I feel close to coming, she stops what she's doing and soothes me with gentle circles of her hand on my bright red skin. I revel in her touch, relaxing each time I'm able to have her close.

But then she's gone once more, and the pain returns.

My whole body is weightless as I lie there only halfway on the bed. Everything is hazy as she paddles me. My head is empty for once and there's no tension in my body at all. My vision glasses over, nothing quite clear enough to truly picture.

I'm her plaything, a toy, something to tease and taunt. Her punishments no longer feel like a burden but a gift. They're something to be thankful for, and I'm grateful for her offering. Nothing has ever felt like this before. I've never experienced this state of being.

All I am is what she's made me.

The bliss lingers along with the spreading fire that burns under my skin, and then her touch is back, rubbing those same circles into my backside.

When her fingers slide into the crease between my cheeks, I freeze. She strokes between them, reaching down to play with my balls before stroking up my perineum and back to the plug. Grabbing the flared base, she pulses it in me. Pressure increases as she pushes the plug just a little deeper inside me and releases when she pulls back.

"Please, Mistress. I'm so close," I beg breathlessly. "I need to come, please. Please."

I'm leaking pre-cum and whining like a pup. My hands grip the sheets as I'm desperately trying to keep from thrashing around.

"Look how pretty you are, leaking onto the floor. Such a messy mutt," Mistress coos.

Her hand comes around to grasp me by the shaft, and the warmth brings me closer to the edge. She grips me tightly as she gives me a few pumps, drawing mindless pleas from my lips.

But I'm too close, and she hasn't given me permission. It's

like she's trying to get me to disobey. She's taunting and teasing me, forcing me to my limit for her satisfaction of seeing me squirm.

She releases the plug, and I hope for a moment to collect myself, but then she commands, "Do. Not. Come."

With each word, three hard strikes of her hand land on my ass, and lightning shoots through me. Every nerve in my body is thrumming with energy as my cum jets through my shaft and out on the floor, but my release brings me both heavenly bliss and humiliation.

The sticky substance leaks from my tip, a string of cum grounding me back to reality. My breathing is heavy, and shame clouds me as I realize what I've done.

I didn't heed her instructions. I failed to obey.

"Oh." She pouts, grabbing me by the root of my hair and forcing me to the floor.

I waver on my knees a bit, but she steadies me with her free hand before shoving my head down. "Someone's made a mess, haven't they?" She pushes me to all fours. "Lick it up."

Staring at the mess before me, I contemplate disobeying once more. I've never done anything like this before. It feels both so wrong and yet so enticing. It's the more significant part of me, the part that's satiated and free, which I want to submit.

I bend my elbows, getting close to the ground, and give a brief glance up at her. Her expression is hidden softness. She's not asking me to do this against my will but because I'm choosing to let her direct my desire.

Leaning down more, I open my mouth and stretch out my tongue. The carpet is scratchy as I lick the floor, but the salt of my own cum hits me full force. Gagging a little at the sheer volume I produced, I continue to lick up the mess until it's gone.

When I lean back onto my heels, I look at her.

"Say thank you, dog," she says, her voice soft yet firm. "Say it." I can tell by the tenseness in her eyes it was a mistake to let her tell me twice.

My pulse picks up at the fire in her eyes, the need I can so clearly see in her.

"Thank you, Mistress," I say, staring up at her from the floor.

There's a sparkle in her eye and a smile on her lips when she grabs me by the leash tethered to my neck and pulls me to a kneeling position.

Her fingers come to my temple and comb into my hair. The movement is delicate and comforting, making me lean into her hand further.

"You really are bad, aren't you? You can't help but break every rule you're given," she admonishes. "You really shouldn't have done that. I'm the one who decides when you get to come. Aren't I?"

Guilt wracks me at the knowledge that I have, once more, disappointed her. "Sorry, Mistress."

Tears well at the corner of my eyes, and I fight to hold them back. The bliss from release and peace from my punishment has broken down the protective walls I keep around myself.

"Mmmh. So many apologies tonight, and yet all of them feel empty," she says, wiping away my tears. "Do they feel empty to you, mutt? Is your word just as worthless as you are?"

Her words hurt so good. They're unlocking something in me, and hearing her call me such awful things has me hardening once more despite having just come without permission.

"No. I mean them," I say softly.

"Mean what, exactly?"

I try to put words together to express my sincerity, but they escape me. My tongue fumbles as my heart clenches from knowing she deserves so much more than my pitiful silence.

Finally, I gather myself enough to speak. "I've done wrong by you," I confess. "I don't deserve the time or energy or attention you pay me. I am a disappointment and a failure. I'm not enough for you, and yet, you're here."

There's a moment of stunned silence between us, both from her, not expecting my confession, and from me, unaware I was capable of this kind of honesty. But seeing her melt before me makes the vulnerability worth it.

"Color," she says, her voice turning to steel.

"Green," I reply enthusiastically.

A grin spreads across her face. "Good. Because I'm not done with you yet, and if you're going to come without permission, then I'm going to milk them out of you until you're dry."

Taking me by my leash, she yanks me up until I'm standing. Our gazes connect, and I stare into the starlight in her eyes.

My cock jumps when she touches me. Part of me is relieved when she reaches for the ring, still encasing my cock and balls. Another part is already missing the vice it has around me, knowing it's been a constant reminder of her ownership. Then, she pushes me back on the bed.

In her pink lingerie and heels, she looks so dainty, but the ice in her expression says I'm in for a world of torment. Her slow steps have me moving back farther onto the bed until I'm pressed up against the headboard. She's a panther as she crawls toward me, each graceful movement elongated to draw her prey in. And I would go with her willingly, too.

Holding herself above me, she stoops down and gives my head a slow lick before taking it into her mouth. I revel in her heat as she sucks on my sensitive tip, and I can feel the same tingle at the base of my cock once more.

Her mouth pauses just above me, and she pools her saliva before spitting it onto my head, the vision reminding me of earlier and the way she spits on me like I was nothing to her. This time, there's a reverence to the way she takes me in hand and strokes me up and down.

The combination of her hand and mouth on me is driving me to the edge. Pressure builds in my straining shaft until I'm so close to coming it is painful.

"Please, Mistress. Can I come?" I beg, my hips bucking up off the bed and driving me deeper into her throat.

She takes me so well, and even amongst the haze of pleasure and my need for release, I recognize what an honor it is for her to give me this moment.

"Please . . . I . . . I need . . ."

Backing off me, she brings herself up to a kneeling position and releases me.

"You want to come?"

I nod frantically.

"Then do it yourself. Show me how you stroke yourself to completion. I'm going to watch as you fall apart for me."

I don't need her to tell me twice.

My cock is in my hand in a second, and I squeeze it tightly, adding just the right amount of pressure to the base. I glide my hand up and down my shaft, rolling my wrist each time I get to the head, but it's the light scratch of my mistress's nails along my inner thighs which have me crashing into bliss.

Cum spills out of me and onto my chest, some even managing to land on my neck. The white substance dots my body, standing out against my tanned skin.

"What a good boy," Mistress says, swiping some of my cum up with her fingers. "Now taste."

Her fingers come to my lips, and I willingly open wide.

Taking my come from her fingers is so much more rewarding than licking it from the floor. Yet, I know if she demanded it of me, I would do it again and again. I lick her fingers clean until the taste of myself is gone, and all that's left is the ambrosia of my mistress.

She pulls her fingers from my mouth, and I chase after them, leaning forward and hoping for more of her. But her hands are at her side, and her gaze is on my quickly softening cock.

"Oh, pet. Don't give up on me now. You are capable of so much more," she says, leaning down to give my head a kiss, which has it jerking in response.

She moves to get off me and strolls to the table full of goodies with a satisfying swing to her hips. My head collapses against the headboard, and my eyes flutter close as I try to collect my breath.

When I open my eyes once more, my mistress is standing beside the bed, plugging a wand into the plug in the nightstand.

She sets the wand down beside me, only to pick up a pair of cuffs I hadn't noticed lying on the bed before. A silent motion has me holding out my wrists to her, and I marvel at the ease of quiet communication that flows between us. The whole process of binding my wrists into the leather cuffs occurs with practiced ease.

She buckles the last cuff around my wrist before clipping them together with a chain, which she then uses to push my hands above my head. She's so close now I can feel the heat of her breath on me. Her plush lips are close enough for me to kiss, and I yearn for the connection, but she stays still.

I want more, need more, but I'm already pushing my body to my limit, and I don't know if I can take any more of her attention. Every one of my nerves is already electrified with her touch, and part of me feels like anything more will leave me completely wrecked.

Pulling back from above me, she takes the wand into her hand. She sits there on the side of the bed and looks me in the eyes before turning it on. The buzz of the toy makes my body tighten as she brings the bulb closer to my tip, and I can't help but squirm in anticipation.

When it makes contact with the head, I cry out, but this time not in sheer ecstasy but rather in agonizing pain. My cock screams at the vibrations going through my tip. The wand sends a burning sensation up my spine and into my skull, where it reverberates.

I thrash with my eyes shut, trying to keep going, to be good, but it's too much.

"Red!" I cry out, and immediately, everything stops.

The wand turns off, and a sigh of relief escapes me. The cuffs come off with practiced ease, and suddenly, I'm free. Tears burn behind my eyelids and drip down my face.

Her touch is a balm to my soul when she wipes away the tears with her fingertips, but the touch is still too much.

"No," I pant out, hating I can't have her near. "No more. Please."

Her hand withdraws, and I open my eyes to see a shattered, vulnerable woman, but then it's gone, replaced by my confident mistress.

"I'm going to clean you up," she says with authority. "Washcloth or baby wipes?"

I shudder at the thought of a scratchy washcloth on my skin. "Wipes."

"Got it."

Moments later, she's back with the wipes and cleans down my torso. When she reaches my cock, she gives me a look before handing me several.

"Clean yourself up as best you can and take out the plug. Ask if you need help. I'll be right back," she whispers.

Wanting to prove myself a self-sufficient man, I start by working the plug out of me before I can even bring myself to wipe up the saliva and cum on my shaft. When I'm done, she's back at my side, her arms loaded with supplies.

I look at her wide-eyed, but she just shrugs. "Water, protein bars, fuzzy socks, and a weighted blanket."

I drop my jaw, remembering the long conversations we had about each of our responses to overstimulation and aftercare.

"Fuck. No wonder the bag was so heavy." I chuckle.

She gives me a small smile before setting things down on the bed. The movements are like a ritual for her. First, she cracks open the water bottle and holds it for me while I take a few sips. Then, she opens the protein bar before handing it to me, instructing me to take small bites and chew slowly. When she's done fussing with the pillows behind me, she picks up the blanket and drapes it over me.

"I want to hold you . . . ," she admits, sitting back on the edge of the bed. ". . . but I know . . ."

"I'm sorry." I relax as the weighted blanket grounds me.

She looks down at the bedspread and fiddles with one of the stray threads.

"Don't apologize for knowing what you need." She pauses and looks up hopefully. "Can I . . . May I hold your hand?"

I consider for a moment what it would mean for me. She said she always needs physical contact after play. I don't, and right now, it's almost too much for me. But surely, this is a compromise that will be worth it.

"Yeah, we can try that." I smile.

"Thank you." She sighs in relief. "I'll be right back."

I'm already starting to drift off when my mistress comes back in her own fuzzy socks and a soft-looking nightgown. She climbs under the sheets and scootches close to me before reaching the nightstand to grab what looks like a tablet or e-reader.

She reaches under my blanket to wrap her fingers between my own, and I turn to curl closer to her warmth, which makes her smile down at me. "Sleep for a bit, baby. I'll watch over you while you do." She nuzzles into my hair and whispers in my ear, "Thank you for trusting me."

7

———

Mistress

I can't focus on my book, and the feeling of my fingers wrapped in my pet's distracts me.

Part of me is grateful he safed out, but I pushed him too far, and the regret of it all weighs heavily on my chest.

I haven't been a good Domme to him. I've been all over the place emotionally, and it's colored every moment of our time together. I wasn't what I needed to be for him, yet here he is, snoring lightly next to me with my hand clutched in his massive paw. He's giving me the privilege of touching him even after I pushed him too far, and I'm infinitely grateful for that.

Turning away from the one paragraph I've been skimming over and over, I look at my pet where he sleeps. I take in the slope of his nose and the arch of his brows. His cheeks are flushed from our activities, and his lips curve in a slight smile.

The weighted blanket surprised me when we talked about aftercare, but seeing such a big man curled up under the gray covering makes him seem so much smaller and more fragile.

The telltale signs of panic start taking over as I sit there, guilt wrecking me as I take in my vulnerable pet. My head swims as I watch him sleeping peacefully. Breathlessness seizes my lungs, and I clammer to maintain control of my body, but the pressure to cave to my irrational terror is overwhelming.

Switching from my reading application, I go to my texts and type out a quick message.

THURSDAY 3:12 A.M.

B: I need you.

Within minutes, my tablet is ringing, and I pick up, knowing the consequences if I don't.

"Baby, it's late," Durante says groggily.

"Shhh. He's asleep," I whisper. "Give me a second."

My gaze slides to my pet, making my heart clench as I take in how peacefully he sleeps before forcing myself to let go of his hand.

Taking my tablet into the bathroom, I shut the door behind me with a quiet click before sliding down the nearest wall and sitting, scrunched up. My tablet sits on my knees, and when I return to look at Durante's vision on the screen, I cringe.

"You shushed me," he admonishes.

Sir is so handsome, his looks only illuminated by the light of his phone screen. In the darkness, I can still tell his sandy brown hair is rumpled, and there's an imprint from the pillowcase on his cheek.

"Sorry," I say quietly, knowing I've disrespected him by forgetting my position in our dynamic.

My head is still in my Domme mindset, where I have complete ownership over my thoughts, words, and choices. But with my sir, I made the choice to give that over to him.

The dialectic is messing with my head, which I shake to refocus.

"It's alright," he says, rubbing away the sleep persisting in his dark hazel eyes. "He's there, right?"

I take a quick glance at the door. "Yeah, in the bedroom."

"And you've gone and locked yourself in the bathroom?" He smirks knowingly.

"Umm . . . yeah," I admit.

"Any particular reason, baby?" He yawns.

"No . . ."

Yes.

"Are you lying to me?" His amusement is evident in his rough voice. "Sounds like someone needs a spanking when they get home."

I roll my eyes. "Yes, Sir."

Much as I loathe to admit it, I probably do need a good spanking. I've admonished my pet repeatedly tonight for his bad behavior, but mine hasn't been much better.

"Are you going to tell me what's wrong and why you're having me call you at 3 a.m.?"

I stay quiet, not wanting to admit to my own failure.

Between the unexpected actions by my pet and my own swinging emotions, it's been a mess of a day. And yes, I enjoyed myself, but it doesn't feel right. Something is very wrong in my heart, and I need the claustrophobic feeling to go away.

"I . . . ," I whisper.

"Speak up when you address me, baby bird," he says, sitting up in bed and turning on one of our bedside lamps.

Sir's screen jostles a bit as he rises and begins moving around the room. From this new angle, I can see his muscular chest and the slight pudge around his tummy. His body is a perfect representation of my sir, hard and soft at the same time. He's firm for me but gentle when he sets boundaries.

It's only been since yesterday morning, but I miss him.

"Yes, Sir," I reply.

Everything is so mixed up inside me. I don't even know where to start. I thought I was in control and that I was anticipating his needs as we went through the scene, but his "red" caught me off-guard.

When the words left his mouth, I almost hesitated. I almost didn't believe him. Sir has conditioned me to respond to his own safewords when he needs to break a scene, but it's been a while since he's done that. So, it took a second to register what my pet was saying.

I wasn't ready.

"He used his safeword," I say, ashamed.

"Good," Sir praises.

My jaw drops when he brings the camera back up to his face, and I spot his wide smile. He shouldn't be proud of me for this. He should be as ashamed of me as I am of myself.

"What? No. Not good," I say frantically. "What are you talking about? It means I failed him. This is all over before we really even get started. And it's my fault."

"Precious . . ." Sir stops in his tracks and takes a deep breath before letting out a long sigh. "Failure isn't the end. It's the beginning, a first step."

"How can you say that?" I whine, running my hand through my curls.

Nothing about today has been a beginning, or at least not a good one. If this is how things start, then we're doomed.

"Baby, I can hear your brain catastrophizing," he says sweetly as he resumes strolling through our home and turning on lights as he goes.

"I want to come home," I choke out, tears starting to well in my eyes.

"Baby, no. Don't you dare abandon the boy," he says sternly. "Look, I've failed you time and time again. I've never been the perfect partner, but I'm here because I want to be my best self for you."

"Durante . . . ," I start, tears sneaking out from the corners of my eyes that I wipe away quickly, but they won't stop coming.

"Don't 'Durante' me." He laughs softly. "It's true. I've never been enough for you, and that's what keeps me coming back. I'm just as drawn to you as you are to me. And I need you more than I would ever willingly admit to anyone."

It's been such a long time since we first met, and the memories are hazy, but I do remember it taking us a while to find our stride. We had plenty of disagreements, and negotiating was a nightmare in the beginning.

"Baby, he's likely the same. If you want each other, that's the only thing you need to make things work," he says, flicking on the lights in our kitchen.

I'm a waterfall by the time he finishes speaking, and I'm gasping for breath. Ever since the day I first found my pet, I've wanted him. But it didn't seem like enough today.

"But he safed out. He said, red," I say, dread consuming me.

"You stopped and went into aftercare, right?" Sir asks with a knowing tone.

"Well, yeah. Of course. I stopped everything. But like . . . how do you come back from that?"

Sir sets the phone down on the counter before leaving the frame and addressing me. "And he's currently snoring in the bedroom while you're here talking to me?"

"Yes. What's your point?" I bite out.

His head pops back into the screen, and his face is stern. "Don't get snippy with me, miss."

I stay silent, and I'm grateful when he lets my sass slide, though part of me knows I'll pay for it later.

"My point is you did everything you could have done. You did well, baby. Exactly as I've taught you. But you knew that, didn't you?" he says, his voice echoing from somewhere else in the kitchen.

I think back through those last moments of our session. How pet cried out, and I sprang into action. I had everything on hand I needed to take care of him but somehow, it doesn't feel like it was enough. There's supposed to be something more.

"Then what's next?" I ask as the espresso maker percolates in the background.

"What's next is you crawl back into bed with him and take care of him how he needs you to. Then you talk."

"I have a meeting in three and a half hours, and I can't miss it."

"And?" Sir leaves the frame again and returns with a mug in his hands.

"I don't want to wake him," I admit.

"Then don't. Let him sleep. Call his assistant and have them cancel his appointments and meetings. Get room service to bring up breakfast and lunch in case he wakes up hungry. Leave him a note and have him call you. Then you talk. And you keep talking until you've figured this out with him. Got it?" Sir says, as though it's the simplest solution in the world.

Something opens in my chest at the idea, though. "Yes, Sir. That's actually . . . a really good plan."

"I know, precious." He yawns. "You good now?"

"Yeah, thank you." I sigh.

"You're doing great, baby. Invest as much trust in yourself as your pet does in you. You've got this," Sir encourages.

"Thank you, Sir," I say quietly.

"Of course, baby." He pauses. "Take care of what you need to do there, and if you have time, stop by the house. I'll help you get ready and out the door in time."

"Yes, Sir. I can also handle some things from the car," I tell him.

"Good girl," he says sweetly before hanging up.

I sit there for a long time before getting up to throw on clothes and pack my bag with everything from tonight. Then I go about making arrangements for the day, which Sir helpfully put into a shared note for me to check off.

I text Marcus first to ask him to pick me up and receive a prompt reply he will be downstairs in thirty minutes. My pet's assistant, on the other hand, panicked when he picked up when I called his boss's phone, and I felt a little bad for waking him so early. So, I make a note to myself to make sure he gets a thank-you gift. The front desk wasn't very happy to hear from me either when I called down around four a.m. to arrange for food to be brought up to the suite for breakfast and lunch, but I told them to put a massive tip on the bill and hoped it makes up for it.

I'm really hoping all of this makes up for a lot.

I don't want to leave him, especially when I come back to the room and find Pet sprawled on the bed. He's flopped off his side and onto his stomach, arm reaching out to where I was previously and clutching my pillow to his face. Even asleep, he seeks me out, and my heart melts at the gesture.

I go over to the bed and, sit on the edge closest to him and brush some locks of hair from his face. He looks so peaceful there, and I almost hesitate to say goodbye.

"Baby," I say, scratching his back lightly. "I have to go."

He rolls over in my direction with a glassy expression on his face, which makes me doubt he's even fully awake right now.

"I have to go," I repeat and receive a grunt in reply, which has a chuckle escaping me. "Call me when you wake up."

Pet moves closer to me, burying his face into the skirt of my dress, and my fingers go to run through his hair.

"Don't leave yet," he mumbles out.

Something about the request makes my heart clench. In a

moment, I decide I'm keeping him. He's no longer a mutt but my rescue.

"Oh, pet. You've just been looking for someone to save you, huh?"

I lean down and give him a gentle kiss on his forehead, which he tries to follow as I pull away. "Well, you're mine now."

EPILOGUE

Pet

I wake up to the sun pouring through the eastern windows, illuminating the room in a way that starkly contrasts the comforting feeling of dim lights the night before.

Looking around, though, I don't see any trace of my mistress. No clothes are piled neatly in the corner. All the bags from our shopping excursion are missing, along with her own luggage I brought up for her. The emptiness crashes into me, capturing my breath and constricting my heart. Frantically, I jump out of bed, hoping to find any lasting trace of her.

I grab a T-shirt, boxers, and the slacks I brought for traveling, throwing them on, but forego shoes. Quickly, I grab my hotel room key, anxiety building in my chest, and head for the door, but I stop in my tracks at the sight of a lilac and cream card on the entryway table.

The weight of the card in my hand, the one she took back from me and said I must earn once more, brings air back into my lungs. But it's not until I notice the perfect penmanship on the back, though, that I finally calm my racing heart.

Check your email. - M

Card tight in my grasp, I stride to the bedside table where my phone is charging. Sure enough, a notification pops up on my screen.

You're going to Edinburgh on 12/30 (3ZEKPA)! Here's your itinerary and receipt.

I push down the hope temporarily before switching to my contacts and bringing her up. I tap to call her, but it rings all the way through. So, again, I tap the call icon and wait for her to pick up.

"It's almost noon. You slept in," she says, her sultry voice making my cock perk up once more.

I smirk at the smile in her voice. "Someone wore me out last night. When did you leave?"

"Around 7 a.m. I had a morning meeting, but you sleep like the dead," she says. "And I couldn't take any more of your snoring."

"I do *not* snore," I scoff.

"You're right. You purr like a lion, then."

Light laughter comes through the phone before silence falls between us. Immediately, my whole body relaxes, tightness and terror fleeing at once at the sound of her giggling. Last night, we both went to extremes. It was pure tension and passion. Her radiance pulled me into her, but my rebellion pushed me away. It's good to have this back, this lightheartedness between us.

"I got an email," I say, my voice quieter than before, less sure.

"Correct."

I hesitate. "It's a plane ticket."

"Once again, you are correct." Her tone has a particular clip to it, which worries me.

I want her to confess, to tell me what it all means. Share what her intentions are. I have a gut feeling, but I need her to say the words out loud. Those three little words.

"It's to Edinburgh. Over the New Year's holiday."

My palms sweat at the possibility she wants to spend the new year together.

She wants to *start* the new year together.

"Yes," she says.

That . . . *she wants me.*

"That's in four months."

"You really are catching on, aren't you?" I can hear the smirk in her voice, but the agitation from earlier is gone, and our play continues.

I chuckle. "So, you're planning on making me wait four months before I can see you again?"

Her intake of breath through the phone has me clearly picturing her closing her eyes to take a moment to center herself. "I waited for you, Symon."

Silence comes through the line, and the world fades away. I clench my fists, knowing I brought this upon myself. I'm the problem. This is on me.

I cut her out for so long, and I can only imagine the roller coaster of feelings she went through. Was she angry with me? Disappointed? Did she cry in my absence?

Regret constricts my chest, and my breathing shallows. I wipe my hands against my jeans, trying to get rid of the sweat caused by my anxiety.

"So there's no chance I can see you before then?" I choke out. "I . . . I didn't give you your gift."

"Tribute," she corrects.

"Right. Tribute." I stand and cross to where my suitcase lies and pick out the blue velvet box from the bijou jewelry shop. "I want to give it to you, but I don't want to wait four months. My heart can't take it. It belongs to you."

My words hang in the air, their dual meaning heavy in the silence.

"Then you'll just have to work on your patience," she says, redirecting the conversation.

"Yeah, that's not my virtue."

Box in hand, I sit on the bed, staring at them like they have answers to questions I haven't even thought of yet.

"I know." She's back to laughing. "You're eager. It's cute. Mr. Big-time CEO who's used to having everything he wants, waiting around for little ol' me."

"You are little, though."

"Hey! I'm 4'11". *You're* the giant in this relationship," she says emphatically.

"Relationship, Reka?"

Voices in the background filter through the phone.

"Give your assistant a couple of weeks off over the holidays. I kinda woke him up early this morning, and he was panicking." She rushes out her response, and my anxiety returns. "I have to go."

"Reka, please."

"I have a meeting. I need to go. See you in the new year, Symon."

The phone call ends and shock takes over. All I can concentrate on is the hum of the air being pushed through the vents. The ticking of the wall clock is the only thing keeping me breathing. In for ten, hold, then push the air out. Repeat.

I fall back against the bed, curl up on my side, and drag the weighted blanket over me once more. It's not until the clock chimes three times that I snap out of my stupor. I've already missed all my meetings for the day. There's no point in getting out of bed at this point.

But I roll over to my other side and spot the velvet box once more and am compelled to move. I pick them up and undo the clasps, keeping each of them shut and placing the now open boxes on the comforter.

Opening the box reveals a simple silver bracelet fastened in the center with a small ribbon. Attached to the chain is a matching silver training clicker, which glints in the light as I pick it up.

I don't spot it at first among the delicate filigree on the silver surface, but once I see it, I can't drag my eyes away. The engraving steals my breath.

Property of M

She knew. Even before I did, she knew. And her certainty makes my heart flutter.

Your obedience is my real gift. Nothing compares to your submission. Just as I am hers, she is mine. She's my everything. My sunshine and light. My reason for being.

I HOPE YOU ENJOYED *HEEL*! If you're looking for more kinky romance to read, check out the The Playground Club series. It begins with *Bound*, a spicy FFM romance with a cowboy who's *very* good with rope!

Get your copy!

To stay up to date on news, sales, and releases from Shannon Elliot, join her newsletter here:

Join the newsletter!

ACKNOWLEDGMENTS

This has been the messiest and most chaotic project I've written to date. I cannot be more grateful to everyone who contributed to this project and helped make it become what it is now.

Becca W., wifey, I love you to the moon and back. Our friendship means the world to me and I would not have made it through this project without your encouragement and support. You're my rock and I'm incredibly honored to call you my friend. Tell Hubby he's a trooper for putting up with your side piece.

Becca Fogg, I absolutely adore you. You're the organized to my chaos and the calm to my storm. This wouldn't have happened without you. Thank you for being my friend and Jewish mom.

Emily, your contributions to this project completely changed how I craft stories, and I cannot be more appreciative. Thank you for pushing me and encouraging me.

Bex, thank you for stepping in when I needed you and keeping me going. Your reassuring words made all the difference. Thank you for being my friend.

Ashley, you're a grounding presence in my life. Your wisdom knows no bounds and you have fundamentally changed me as a human, made me better. Thank you for being you.

To my betas, Bria, Nika, Shani, and Tuesday, thanks for taking the time to read and give me the giggles. I love y'all's feedback and I'm so grateful for your contributions to this project.

To my group chat, y'all are my ride or dies. I love every one of you endlessly. Thank you for putting up with me and inspiring me to be my most authentic self.

Norma, you're a gem and I will always appreciate you for your incredibly high level of work, but also your enthusiasm. Also, for putting up with me in general.

To my family, I love you. This book marks the beginning of a new era in Shannon's World, and I could not do this without you. Thank you for believing in me and supporting me. Thank you for being mine.

ABOUT THE AUTHOR

Shannon Elliot resides in Houston, TX, with her fur baby and writes romance that reflects her readers whenever she's not at the dog park dog or curled up with a good book. Evidenced by her background in theatre, she is drawn to story-telling and the creative process. Shannon believes that diverse and inclusive stories shouldn't be the exception, they should be the rule. Happily ever after is for everyone and she aims to write romances that reflect her readers.

Visit the Website

ALSO BY

<u>The Playground Club</u>

Bound, Book 1

Used, Book 2

<u>Descent into Darkness</u>

Angels in the Dark, Book 1

Devil in the Dark, Book 2

Standalone Novellas

Heel